ISLANDS AND CONTINENTS

T0083524

Hong Kong University Press thanks Xu Bing for writing the Press's name in his Square Word Calligraphy for the covers of its books. For further information, see p. iv.

ISLANDS AND CONTINENTS

Short Stories by Leung Ping-kwan

Edited by *John Minford*
with *Brian Holton* and *Agnes Hung-chong Chan*

香港大學出版社
HONG KONG UNIVERSITY PRESS

Hong Kong University Press
14/F Hing Wai Centre
7 Tin Wan Praya Road
Aberdeen
Hong Kong

ISBN 978-962-209-844-2

Secure On-line Ordering
http://www.hkupress.org

British Library Cataloguing-in-Publication Data
A catalogue record for this book is available from the British Library.

Printed and bound by Pre-Press Ltd.

Hong Kong University Press is honoured that Xu Bing, whose art
explores the complex themes of language across cultures, has written
the Press's name in his Square Word Calligraphy. This signals our
commitment to cross-cultural thinking and the distinctive nature of
our English-language books published in China.
"At first glance, Square Word Calligraphy appears to be nothing more
unusual than Chinese characters, but in fact it is a new way of
rendering English words in the format of a square so they resemble
Chinese characters. Chinese viewers expect to be able to read Square
word Calligraphy but cannot. Western viewers, however are surprised
to find they can read it. Delight erupts when meaning is unexpectedly
revealed."

— Britta Erickson, *The Art of Xu Bing*

Contents

Foreword
'PK'

■ *John Minford*

Over the years I have noticed people experiencing some difficulty when deciding how to address the author of these stories. For a start, there is the dilemma of whether to use the pen-name he has adopted as an author of fiction and prose, Yah See; or his more formal name as a poet, scholar and teacher — Leung Ping-kwan. Then again, these names themselves can be read either in their original Cantonese (as above), or in Mandarin, the lingua franca of the new Empire, in which case they become respectively Yesi,[1] and Liang Bingjun (this last looks deceptively like a Mainland writer, and very

---

[1] It sounds like the English 'Yes'. I always thought this pen-name originated with the progressive rock band of the 1970s, since PK was very interested in the underground culture of that period. But he informs me: 'As for Yesi, I started writing as a high school student and was too shy to want people to know that I wrote. Also in HK, people considered you crazy if they knew you were a poet! And it was popular to use pen-names in those days. But most of my contemporaries were using very sentimental or romantic pen-names, things like "red leaf", "setting sun", "drizzle", "lonely soul", "wandering soul" etc. I did not like that, I didn't want to have a name with a ready-made meaning, borrowed from some well-developed idea, like a suit of old clothes from relatives. I thought of myself as modern, and a rebel, so I picked two characters from a classical poem I was reading, words with no clear meaning when put together, and I juxtaposed them to form my name. I guess I wanted to give my own meaning to the characters by using them!'

un-Hong Kong). All of which is extremely confusing. For me, he has always been — as friend, poet and story-teller — just plain PK.[2] I believe that PK himself relishes the irony, the fake nostalgia, of this colonial naming device when applied to a post-colonial such as himself. It is a phenomenon true to the wonderfully complex spirit of Hong Kong, this maddening and yet lovable city that he celebrates (and laments) in so many of these stories!

It was only relatively recently that I became aware of another undercurrent in the name PK. There is a Cantonese slang expression *puk gaai*, meaning literally 'hit the street', roughly the equivalent of 'drop dead', or 'piss off, you bastard', and occurring in such coarse expressions as *diu neih louh mou go puk gaai jai* — 'fuck-your-mother's drop-down-dead boy'.[3] The Cantonese-speakers of Hong Kong (ruthless hybridizers of linguistic conventions and indulgers in code-shifting) commonly abbreviate *puk gaai* into the simpler PK. PK himself is proudly Cantonese, and no doubt takes a secret delight in the street-blasphemous Cantonese overtone encrypted into his colonial appellation, with its hint of the 'no-hoper', the 'loser', the person destined (despite his best efforts) to drop dead on the street. This is the sort of character he returns to again and again. His stories are un-selfpitying celebrations of failure. *Why do I always forget? Why can I never find the words?* ('Postcolonial Affairs of Food and the Heart') Or they are gentle chronicles of the wounded, unsuccessful lover. *There's the distance between us, between you and me, which has varied with time. I don't know if I can ever transcend that distance, I don't know if somehow one day I can cross that border.* ('Borders') His postcolonial world is filled with anti-heroes, with 'marginaux', people 'going downhill' — like Lao Ho, the history lecturer in 'Postcolonial Affairs'. *He's started losing some of his hair in the past few*

---

[2] If we were to universalize this usage, whereby the initial letters of the personal name are used to create a 'Western' name, the late unlamented Chairman Mao (Mao Tse-tung) would become T. T. Mao, Premier Zhou Enlai would become E. L. Zhou, Deng Xiaoping would turn into X. P. Deng, etc.

[3] See Christopher Hutton and Kingsley Bolton, *A Dictionary of Cantonese Slang* (Honolulu, 2005), p. 95.

years. He hasn't been able to withstand this inescapable part of historical necessity. I've known him for many years, and I've watched him going steadily downhill. Or like the writer's lonely friend in 'Islands and Continents', a man haunted by his failed love affair, by the torture of his infatuation — *quite incapable of any normal transaction with the world.*

The word 'marginal' is in a sense the key to this book. PK sees himself as marginal: marginal to the academic world and the city in which he works to earn a living — *pushed out to the margins of a closed community*; marginal to the 'greater Chinese' context to which he supposedly 'belongs'. *Where should I stand in the sculpture garden? In the centre or on the periphery? Should I sit cradled in the arms of a giant statue? Or should I watch from the edge…* ('Borders') Hong Kong itself (*the commercially-minded society of this small border island*) is a place on the margins, a border town, an island, as opposed to a, or the, continent (or mainland).[4] There is a recurring tug-of-war between the grandeur of the 'motherland', and the proudly independent voice of Hong Kong, a paradoxical relationship between border towns like Hong Kong and Shenzhen, and the huge mass of China. *Somewhere behind the transitional shabbiness of Shenzhen, there was also a certain magnificence to China.* ('The Dentists on the Avenida de la Revolución') This is the dual landscape of his stories, a fluctuating, insecure world, where islands and continents co-exist: *all the little islands and hills, stretching into the distance… and behind them, very faint in the background, the mountains of the mainland, the great continent.* ('Islands and Continents')

♣

This book of stories mirrors one that appeared a few years ago in French.[5] It consists of four longer pieces ('Postcolonial Affairs of Food and the Heart', 'Borders', 'Islands and Continents' and 'The Dentists on the Avenida de la

---

[4] In Chinese, the word *lu* or *dalu* can mean either continent (as in the European or American continent) or mainland (as in Mainland China). This important ambiguity is impossible to reproduce in English.

[5] *Îles et Continents et autres nouvelles*, translated by Annie Curien, Paris, Gallimard, 2001.

Revolución');[6] two shorter, and more light-hearted, or surreal, stories ('The Romance of the Rib', and 'Transcendence and the Fax Machine'), and the even shorter 'cameo', 'Postcards from Prague'. The collection acquaints the reader with contemporary Hong Kong's most eloquent voice, a writer whose gentle humour is shot through with a lingering sense of melancholy, and whose involvement in serious intellectual and cultural issues is tempered by a childlike and engaging naïvety. It may be helpful here to round out the acquaintance by placing some of PK's poetry beside his fiction.[7] The poetry can provide an illuminating counterpoint, sometimes echoing the humour, sometimes drawing out the subdued lyricism, sometimes exploring the intellectual preoccupations. Here, for example, are two very recent, unpublished lyrics, sent last week from snowbound Cambridge. They show him writing in his minimalist, intimate style, echoing the folk lyrics of the ancient *Book of Songs*.

Marsh Mulberry

On the street between redbrick houses,
So many umbrellas, so many colours;
Suddenly I ran into you,
And around us the colours shone so bright.

On the road spotted with rain,
Damp reflections of lamplight.
Suddenly I found you,
And the light held words that couldn't be said.

---

[6] An earlier draft of the translation of 'Postcolonial Affairs of Food and the Heart' appeared in the US Quarterly *Persimmon*, in 2001. Similarly, an earlier version of Caroline Mason's translation of 'Islands and Continents' (under a different title, 'The Island and the Mainland') appeared in the Hong Kong publication, *China Perspectives*, no. 30, July/August 2000.

[7] There are two books of English translations available: *City at the End of Time (1982), and Travelling with a Bitter Melon* (2002). Otherwise there is a selection of early poems in the Hong Kong Special Issue of *Renditions*, 29-30, 1988 (pp. 210-221), and a more recent selection in *West Coast Line*, a journal of Simon Fraser University (1997).

On the street of fresh snow,
Patches of black and white.
Suddenly I found you.
And around us the cars sounded so distant.

In the drizzle the street-lamps flared;
Why don't they spew out their fire?
Perhaps it's best to store it,
A little warmth each day for the heart.

Sun in the East

Sunlight shines through the eastern window.
The tea's warm; in the hall, shelves of books
Tumble from ancient dynasties, pell-mell into the room.
We leaf through them, hoping to find some little thing.
You move closer, lightly
Your pink socks brush the soles of my feet.

Moonlight shines through the eastern window.
The tea's cold; don't put on the water again,
You say. No end to the reading of books.
Chance discoveries on the page stay longest in the heart.
You stand in the doorway, softly
Your pink socks rest on the soles of my feet.

In the stories in this book, from time to time we encounter this same voice, a quietly observed everyday street setting for a sudden impulse of the heart, a shared chance discovery, some carefully drawn interior montage, where intimacy is slowly and delicately etched, like a scene from a Wong Kar-wai movie, giving us a little warmth each day for the heart.

Back in the mid-1980s, when Mainland China first started exporting its new poets to Hong Kong and the West, PK was already established as one of Hong Kong's leading modernist poets and critics. These lines are from a 1983 poem, 'Leaf Crown', one from a difficult, almost metaphysical series entitled 'Lotus Leaves'.

I wait in faith, to hear
The sepal breath, I am heavy and clumsy,
Thwarted by mud. You drift lightly across the water
Shedding the petals of yesterday, a fresh clean face again
In a public world, gaining wide circulation.
My leaves and stalks have their share of hubbub too, but
Are muddy, sluggish, caught in private nightmares and
Perilous deluges of dawn, and my roots, tangled
In silt, can never make themselves clear…[8]

During those years, as Hong Kong's own future became uncertain, and China embarked hesitantly on its new chapter of 'reform' (to be cut short so brutally in June 1989), PK welcomed the young newcomers from the long-frozen North with characteristic generosity. It was in the presence of members of that Volant Tribe of Bards from the Mainland that I first encountered him.[9] Even at that early juncture, the tension between his brand of home-grown (if European- and US-educated) modernism, and the more tormented trajectory of Mainland Chinese modernism, reborn from the ashes of the Cultural Revolution, was clearly discernible. The contrast between the cultural environments of the 'island' and the 'continent', the conflicting demands of a deep feeling for the land and literature of his ancestors, and the questioning, questing free spirit of the soon-to-be-returned colony, were to become recurring themes in much of his work. They are strongly present, for example, in the semi-autobiographical story 'Borders'.

Later, in the 1990s, as Hong Kong came to terms with its new identity as a Special Administrative Region of China, I spent many enjoyable hours with PK in various bars across the territory, going over drafts of translations, plotting events together. One of these events was in London in 1997, a two-

---

[8] *Renditions*, Hong Kong Special Issue (1988), p. 212

[9] Among others, Yang Lian (now resident in London), and Gu Cheng (whose death in 1993 deprived contemporary Chinese poetry of one of its most authentic voices). The term 'Volant Tribe of Bards' is taken from the Renditions Special Issue of 1984, where the 'tribe' of Misty poets was first introduced to a Western readership.

man-show on the South Bank devoted to Hong Kong culture. That summer was a poignant juncture for PK, as Hong Kong approached the grand Handover ceremony (what Prince Charles has so cleverly called the Great Chinese Take-away). For the South Bank PK wrote a poem, in which he 'spoke' to Sir Cecil Clementi, a former Hong Kong Governor and author of the extraordinary Kiplingesque 'Hong Kong Rhapsody', written in 1925:

> Grandly here the Master Builder's power
> Crowns the work of England in Cathay.[10]

At first, in his Response to Clementi, PK expresses his ambivalent relationship to his own colonial past;

> See how hard I have to try
> To squeeze myself into your foreign rhyme!
> For years I've had to stammer like this
>   In your borrowed tongue!
> So what do I feel now? Indifference?
> Or a strange nostalgia?

Then he turns to speak to the new mandarin masters from the North.

> An older rhetoric
> Takes the measure of us now
> Trusses us up
> In the strong calligraphy of tradition,
> Condescends to dribble a drop of casual scholar's ink
> And there we are — cultural waifs… [11]

---

[10] Cecil Clementi, Governor of Hong Kong from 1925 to 1930, had earlier (1905) translated the Cantonese Love Songs of Zhao Ziyong. Clementi was an interesting man of letters, and instrumental in establishing Chinese Studies at the University of Hong Kong. He was sarcastically attacked by Lu Xun in 1927, after his visit to Hong Kong.

[11] The poem is contemporary with the story 'Postcolonial Affairs of Food and the Heart'.

Another (more enjoyable) event took place the following year at the Hong Kong Visual Arts Centre. PK wrote some lighter poems to accompany an avant-garde fashion show, designed by his young friend, Wessie Ling. (PK loves to involve himself with designers, artists, photographers, film-makers, chefs, musicians, dancers…) One of the poems at the 'post-modern' fashion show was simply entitled 'Barbie Doll'.

I'm a Barbie doll
Living in a Barbie city…
Ken is always at the other end of my mobile phone,
Saying, 'You're not happy!
Let's go have some fun together!'
I love the PLA hunks,
I fancy all men in uniform,
Their leather boots turn me on…
I'm a Barbie doll
Visiting a Barbie Legco…

It is the same bright, glittering, evanescent world so well described in 'Postcolonial Affairs', another Handover piece. PK evokes more vividly than any writer I know the shifting sands of Hong Kong's urban mythology, and the stoical courage that enables its 'cultural waifs' to 'have some fun' in the face of such insecurity.

Side by side with his post-modern mask, part serious, part playful, PK has increasingly taken on another persona, that of the timeless Chinese scholar-poet, a laughing, latterday Zen layman, slightly dishevelled, one foot on the path to enlightenment, the other foot trudging worldwearily through the Red Dust. Sometimes (as I have told him more than once) he makes me think of lines by the eighteenth-century Manchu lyricist Nalan Xingde:

Heart burned to ash,
Hair intact,
Not yet totally a monk;
Wind and rain have worn me down.
Here, at this life-death parting,

Lone candle,
I seem to know you.
It's my heart stands between me
And enlightenment.[12]

More and more, PK travels internationally, and writes as a citizen of the world, as part of world culture. During the early weeks of 2005, he wrote a short poem in response to the devastation of the Asian Tsunami, entitled 'A Taste of Asia'. Its poignant understatement gives it the feel of a classical Chinese poem:[13]

The jar you sent had just arrived, stood unopened,
When grim tidings blew in on the grey clouds
From the coast north of you. The earth's contractions
Have brought forth a tsunami. Hotel swallowed in an instant.
Train thrown from its tracks, continuing derailed, driverless
On a journey from this life to the next.
Ocean suddenly overhead. Human lives
Oilslicked and black, flotsam doors, provisions adrift, homeless…

I open the tightly-sealed jar. Pickled garlic.
What is this taste? Bitterness
Buried deep in layers of mud? Harshness of trees torn apart?
Stench of ocean, shattered coral, fish floating belly-up?
What does it mean, your message, wafted my way this sunny afternoon?
Something brewing in the dark? Something growing in turmoil?
Pity and cruelty, glimpsed in the heaving motions of nature?
Can a drop of sweetness temper the infinite brine of this world's woe?

But still, whether as a participant in international gatherings, in Paris, Berlin and New York, or in his continuing dialogue with other Chinese writers from the Mainland, Taiwan and the exile community, PK remains the proud

---

[12] Nalan Xingde, *Nalan ci jianzhu* (Shanghai, Guji, 2003), p. 170.
[13] See for example the Tang dynasty poet Bo Juyi's early poem 'The Charcoal-Seller', in Minford and Lau, *Chinese Classical Literature*, vol. 1, pp. 874-5.

representative voice of Hong Kong. In late 2005, by a strange coincidence, there were two literary events on the same day in Hong Kong. In the afternoon, the exiled poet from the North, Bei Dao, was talking at Hong Kong University. This was a rather solemn, humourless retrospective, a pretentious public musing on the historical significance of the shortlived magazine Today, published by his group of poets nearly thirty years ago in the years after the end of the Cultural Revolution. At the gathering there was an almost sanctimonious air of reverence. Everything took place in Mandarin. There was a certain condescension towards the audience, coming as they mostly did from the Cantonese-speaking 'Cultural Desert' of Hong Kong. The literary VIPs on stage seemed strangely like exiled party cadres caught in a time warp, nostalgically recreating a Mainland political meeting from the old days. All except for PK, who sat there looking slightly bemused, an outsider at the banquet… *I could tell I'd got it wrong once again. Wrong company, wrong food. It's a mistake I keep on making.* ('Postcolonial Affairs')

Later that same evening, down by the harbour, on the top floor of the old Western Market, a second, very different literary event took place. PK met with a motley group of friends to read his poetry, in Chinese (Cantonese, of course), in various English versions, and in Sayed Gouda's Arabic. The atmosphere was very relaxed and good-humoured. There was a generosity of spirit. Good wine was shared. *East and West can cook together, they can merge.* ('Postcolonial Affairs') People wandered around the rooftop site, chatting and looking at the various art objects on display. There was poetry in the air, and a certain amount of spontaneous improvisation. Poetry about food (always one of PK's favourite subjects), short poems celebrating everyday life, bittersweet evocations of relationships gone astray, cameos of the Hong Kong alternative fashion world, wry protests at the pompous rigmarole of politics. There were even ironic references to the 1997 Handover, now eight years in the past, not a heavy-handed retrospective, but the heartfelt expression of an ongoing, private reluctance to be co-opted.

Your proclamations sit heavy on the stomach,
Destroy the appetite;
The table is altogether overdone.
May I be permitted to abstain
From the rich banquet menu,
To eat my simple fare, my gruel, my wild vegetables,
To cook them, to share them with you?[14]

PK's poems and the rooftop readings, along with the traffic sounds from the fly-over just outside the window, were very much part of the rich texture of Hong Kong cultural life — as were the lack of overt importance and the apparent absence of a Party Secretary to spy on the political leanings of those present.

China has a grand literary tradition. Unfortunately, during the twentieth century politics has distorted every branch of human creative endeavour in China, not least the weaving of illusion that is the writing of fiction, and the difficult, sensitive activity that calls itself poetry. Ever since the early decades of the last century, it is China that has been a 'Cultural Jungle', where only a few tough cultural goannas have survived. Hong Kong, by contrast, has quietly preserved and cultivated a space in which the 'spontaneous overflow of powerful feelings' is still possible.

This is the space within which PK functions so well, leaving his readers with a poignant sense of the soul beneath the hard surface of Hong Kong, not afraid to descend on occasions to its darkest depths. *Don't be surprised if I don't write again. Once the light is off, I am the nameless chaos, I am the writhing in the dark, the multitude of things buried beneath the ordered light of day, of things lost in the relations of normal life.* But despite the darkness, there is a human tenderness, a fierce affirmation of individuality. *There, in that darkness, I possess my own imaginary world, a world that is both independent and strangely fruitful.* ('Islands and Continents') It is a warmth,

---

[14] From the poem 'Cauldron'.

a precious, hard-won optimism, that he shares generously with friends and readers. As he puts it in the final sentences of 'Postcolonial Affairs of Food and the Heart' (my personal favourite of the stories in this collection): *Somehow we manage to stay together. Maybe in the end we learn to be kind to one another.... It's late at night now. Outside the streets are empty and desolate. But we can still sit in here, we can linger awhile amid the lights and voices, drunk on the illusion of this warm and joyous moment.*

PK left Hong Kong some weeks ago for a six month spell in the US, just as I was finally sitting down to write this (long overdue) foreword. He has wandered off the map again... The floating world of this city feels strangely empty without him. He is probably in a warm library in Cambridge, busy writing another story or poem, taking refuge from the snows of the North American winter, revising some unfinished manuscript that he has trundled across yet another border, or replying to letters delivered to a previous address. *A hopeless case, a wanderer by nature, a man who enjoys crossing borders and as a consequence often ends up alone like this, an orphaned ghost without a home. Always one step behind reality.* ('Borders')

Hong Kong

Acknowledgements

We acknowledge the contributions made by the translators, who brought this book into being, and heartily thank them for their work. We are also grateful to the Centre for Translation Studies at the Hong Kong Polytechnic University and to Professor Chu Chi-yu, Director of the Centre, for lending us their support and assistance. Above all, we would like to thank Colin Day of Hong Kong University Press for his enduring patience with this long-drawn-out project.

The following lists the publications where the stories collected in this volume were originally published in Chinese and where some of the English translations were first published. Acknowledgement is due to their publishers for their kind permission to reprint materials.

Transcendence and the Fax Machine:
Originally published as 超越與傳真機 in《布拉格的明信片》(*Postcards from Prague*), Hong Kong: Youth Bookstore, 1990, 2000.
The English translation first published in *Running Wild: New Chinese Writers*, New York: Columbia University Press, 1994.

The Romance of the Rib:
Originally published as 肋骨演義 in《布拉格的明信片》(*Postcards from Prague*), Hong Kong: Youth Bookstore, 1990, 2000.

The Dentists on the Avenida de la Revolución:
Originally published as 革命大道路旁的牙醫 in《島和大陸》(*Islands and Continents*), Hong Kong: Wah Han, 1987; Oxford University Press, 2002.

Postcards from Prague:
Originally published as 布拉格的明信片 in《布拉格的明信片》(*Postcards from Prague*), Hong Kong: Youth Bookstore, 1990, 2000.

Borders:
Originally published as 邊界 in《記憶的城市、虛構的城市》(*Cities Remembered, Cities Imagined*), Hong Kong: Oxford University Press, 1993.

Islands and Continents:
Originally published as 島和大陸 in《島和大陸》(*Islands and Continents*), Hong Kong: Wah Han, 1987; Oxford University Press, 2002.
The English translation first published in *China Perspectives*, 30, July–August 2000, pp. 62–73, under the title 'The Island and the Mainland'.

Postcolonial Affairs of Food and the Heart:
Originally published as 後殖民食物與愛情 in《後殖民食物與愛情》(*Postcolonial Affairs of Food and the Heart*), Hong Kong: Oxford University Press, 2007.
The English translation first published in *Persimmon: Asian Literature, Arts and Culture*, v.1, no.3 (winter 2001), pp.42–57.

Transcendence and the Fax Machine

■ *Translated by Jeanne Tai*

I am thirty-seven years old and single, I work as a research assistant at the Institute for Cultural Research, and I moonlight at an accounting firm. In my spare time I like to read the Bible, the Koran, and Buddhist sutras. My field used to be British and American literature. But with the emergence of a Chinese Studies clique among the local scholars and the importance they attached to bibliographic citations, and since I was never on particularly good terms with these people, I began to find my name and my writings excluded from every bibliography and anthology they had a hand in preparing. As time went by I began to sense the presence of bibliographies everywhere: no matter where I went, no matter what I was doing, there always seemed to be an enormous pen hanging right over me, which, with one fell swoop, would make me vanish into thin air. After that I began reading anything and everything. I even began subscribing to certain French journals, including several that focused on religion and literature. Perhaps people involved in the study of religion are more tolerant and considerate; in any case, I would occasionally send them an unsolicited article, and to my surprise they would always respond.

I have remained single for one reason only: I am not very good at interpersonal relationships. Before the age of thirty-five, I used to idealize every woman I met, seeing only the good points and finding plenty of things to love in each of them. And, of course, it always ended in absolute disaster for me. After thirty-five, by way of compensation, I found faults and shortcomings — many of them — in every female I came across. Under these conditions I no longer fell in love with anyone. My heart was calm and serene, like a placid lake, and I expected to live like this happily ever after.

But something unexpected always happens.

One drizzly evening I was out with my photographer friend Li Biansheng. Over a couple of drinks, I mentioned to him that I had been invited by some French scholars to submit a paper for their upcoming conference on Literature and Transcendence. But corresponding with them by mail was time-consuming and very inconvenient. Biansheng was convinced that the solution to my problem was to get a fax machine. Later, while we were walking around Causeway Bay, both of us feeling kind of light-headed, he suddenly said: 'Wait, weren't you going to buy a fax machine?' And he took me to an electronics appliance store. It was just like what my girlfriends used to tell me: if you wander around aimlessly in Causeway Bay, you'll always end up buying something. Since Ah Sheng knew the manager, it didn't matter that I didn't have a cent on me. By the time I left the store I was no longer lonesome — I was on my way home with my fax machine.

Her looks were nothing out of the ordinary, but somehow they came to be more and more pleasing to my eye, perhaps because I was growing, uh, accustomed to her face. I understand that a fax machine is just an instrument for the facsimile transmission of documents — nothing to make a big fuss over, really. But ever since the day she came home with me, my life changed. When I finished something I was writing I no longer had to wander all over the city looking for a real mailbox among all the toylike receptacles on the street, or stamp my feet in frustration in front of the locked doors of the post office, or dodge trams in my quest for some safe deposit to which I could entrust the bundle of intimate, red-hot confidences I was holding in my hands.

No more would I be condemned to roam all creation like a lost soul, stopping in at some telecommunications centre or the Foreign Correspondents' Club for a temporary respite, a chance encounter; never again would I dread the emptiness of an endless weekend or an idle weekday. Though the world outside might be filled with deception, and communication between people might be fraught with traps for the unwary, I could be certain of at least one thing when I got home: she would always be there, faithfully receiving, transmitting, ingesting, an absolutely trustworthy connection linking me and places far away.

What a comfort it was to insert a piece of paper inside her and to know that its soul would appear on the other side of the world. My beloved written word was now able to stand its ground against the evanescent waves of sound and speech. My most personal musings could be flipped over and, in total privacy, poured into a solitary black earpiece. Even the nastiest customs official was powerless to intercept and examine those electromagnetic waves as they wafted through space. And wonder of wonders, there was even material evidence of my intellectual intercourse with the world of the spirit: afterwards there would always be a corporeal copy for my files — a facsimile record, a faithful fuss-free summary of my various mental odysseys. Even if my memory were to fail me in the future, I would still be able to retrace with certainty the footsteps of my soul.

Furthermore, I was now spared the trials and tribulations of daily living. No longer would I have to listen to someone's sighs over the telephone or watch tears trickling down someone's cheeks. Pettiness and jealousy were less likely to ensnarl me when conveyed on paper. No more would I have to answer calls from cantankerous friends who had the habit of slamming down the phone with a suddenness and vehemence that always left my ears ringing. Indeed, thanks to a simple fax machine, my life had undergone a complete transformation. I could now go to sleep, my mind at ease, and when, in the middle of a dream, I heard her muffled coos and murmurs, they sounded like a soothing lullaby reassuring me that all was well.

Little by little I became quite dependent on her. It had been a long time since I had opened my heart to anyone, but she looked so innocent and guileless it was almost inevitable that she would become my one true friend. At work, caught in the daily skirmishes of office politics, I couldn't help but think of her, of her cheerful and open countenance, of how she seemed to represent a kind of communion that was more genuine, more real. After work I wanted nothing else except to be with her. I would make a plate of spaghetti or a salad and pour myself a glass of red wine, relieved just to be in her company. Together we would listen to some music or watch some television. She was my only support in my dealings with the transcendental world. On days when there were no incoming messages, I would switch on her copier mode and feed her what I had written, and it would be reproduced automatically. Expressions such as 'the concept of transcendence in Romantic poetry' or 'Kant's views on the categorical imperative' would materialize on that special paper bearing her unique scent, and to me it was as though she were voicing her concurrence, perhaps even her compliments, thereby giving my confidence an enormous boost.

Precisely because of all this, our first tiff came as that much more of a blow. Right in the middle of a transmission she abruptly clammed up, as if in silent protest against the synopsis of my paper. Several pages went swishing through the machine all stuck together — did she find my style too verbose? Quickly I picked up my manuscript from the floor and reread it from a new perspective. Yes, perhaps points two and three could be combined, and the middle section on page two could be deleted. Maybe some of the issues were a little too abstract? And the conclusion, yes, it was rather abstruse, especially for the younger generation (I had to keep in mind that my fax machine was the product of a new generation and no doubt shared many of the values and viewpoints of her peers). Or was my conclusion too definite, too dogmatic, or perhaps too distant? So I sat down and revised the whole thing, cutting it down from four pages to three. When I tried sending it again, the first page went through smoothly, but the second one stopped halfway through the machine. I waited for a long time but finally had to redial and feed it through again. In the same way, the third page also stopped in the middle of the transmission, and once more I had to resend the whole page. After it was all over I got the usual message: 'Transmission OK', but I couldn't be absolutely sure that the pages actually arrived where they were supposed to go. Was my machine making some sort of protest by her silence, by going on strike today? I grew nervous and uneasy, and fell to speculating about all sorts of possible reasons for the situation.

After that, things went on pretty much as before, as though nothing unusual had happened — until one day, two or three weeks later, when I tried to send a letter and a bibliography to my usual distant destination. Halfway through the transmission, in the middle of the second page, the machine stopped again. When I pulled out the pages and put them back into the feeder for resending, the paper in the roller began to turn instead: the machine was receiving a transmission from somewhere, abruptly cutting off my heartfelt report. As the paper emerged from the other end and slowly flattened out, I began to see a multitude of messages: people leaving Hong Kong to emigrate, selling their furniture at bargain prices ... used cars for sale ... are you in the market for a reliable maid working by the hour ...*udon* noodles ... freshly husked new rice ... a surcharge on taxi fares. They were like installments of a serial, and the story they were telling was not mine. After reading them over carefully, I was convinced they were not some kind of response sent by my far-off correspondents. Most likely my telephone number had found its way onto a master list somewhere, and I was now being sent the gospel according to some advertising agency or communications company.

A practical joke? Maybe. Then again, maybe not. When these messages began coming through a second time, I thought to myself: could there be some special significance, some larger meaning to my being singled out like this? So I studied these faxes even more closely, examining at length each and every sign, symbol, signifier. There didn't seem to be any connection whatsoever between these messages and the texts that I had sent out previously, but on the other hand, maybe there was. Yet what exactly was the nature of that connection? I read and reread the advertisements as they poured out, one after another, in a seemingly endless stream. As for transmitting my own thoughts — well, by then I couldn't get a word in edgeways.

The whirring and humming finally stopped and the communications from the outside world came to an end, for the time being at least. I picked up the pages I had set aside earlier and was about to feed them into the fax machine when, for some unknown reason, I began to feel a little apprehensive — I couldn't send them on their way without looking them over once more. But having just read all that other stuff, I couldn't help feeling an urge to revise the discussion of my proposed paper that I had in front of me. I couldn't help thinking that it was not concise enough, that it carried too much intellectual baggage and was too idealistic, that as a result it sounded unfocused, a little vague. So I revised it yet again.

But when I faxed my letter to the Abbé in Provence, I inadvertently included an advertising circular for plumbing services. Not only that — when I sent a message to the number on the plumbing ad, asking them not to fax me all that junk mail every day, I included, again inadvertently, the letter I had sent earlier to the French cleric. We all work under excessive pressure and end up leaving everything to the last minute. Well, it wasn't until after I had hastily transmitted both of my communiqués that I realized what a blunder I had made, but by then it was too late. The reactions on both ends were just about diametrically opposed. The lofty scholar-critics expressed their concern and misgiving over what they saw as my inclination to 'superficiality' and 'frivolity', because in their view I had introduced mundane and vulgar conceits into what ought to have been a transcendental reverie. The ad agency's reply was predictably terse and impersonal, but even so I could sense the writer's annoyance at having been accosted with meditations on another world, the inordinate gravity of which seemed to embarrass him or her immensely. The respondent didn't quite know what to say, since there were no words in the world of advertising to express such things. But the frosty tone clearly insinuated that I was a religious fanatic completely out of touch with reality.

The paper was much more difficult to write than I had imagined, more so than was usually the case with conference papers: I was much too entangled in the affairs of this world, and it was next to impossible for me to find an unoccupied corner of my mind in which to regroup and reorganize my otherworldly ruminations. The infighting at the office, my mother's rheumatism, the budget for the next fiscal year that I had to prepare posthaste — I was under so much pressure I could hardly breathe. With the deadline for the submission of papers looming just ahead, one after another the clergymen and the professors sent me anxious faxes asking why I hadn't been heard from in so long. Racking my brains, I laboriously composed an abject, mealymouthed reply explaining my situation. When I punched in the number for the transcontinental call, however, the machine emitted a loud beep but never got through to the other end. It was as if I had sent a series of signals to a planet in a distant galaxy, only to find that, in traversing the intervening vortices of light and shadow and colour and sound, my message had somehow gone astray and eventually disappeared without a trace.

I stayed up several nights in a row; even so, I barely managed to finish my first draft the day after the deadline. There were still a few footnotes that had to be checked and several points in the body of the paper that needed further elucidation, but I was already exhausted. Dragging my bone-weary body to the fax machine, I glanced up at the clock on the wall and realized that it was half past four in the morning.

Slowly and tenderly I inserted my manuscript — still warm to the touch, perhaps from the heat of my exertions — into the machine, taking care not to cause her any pain or discomfort. I caressed her dainty, delicate buttons as I gently moved the sheets of paper in and out of the feeder. Afterwards, I leant over her, waiting quietly, hoping fervently that nothing would go wrong this time. I prayed that my message would get through to them, and theirs to me. I longed for the moment when the short, shrill notes of her calling mode would modulate into the rapturous and blissful cadences of contact, coupling, communication. In my quest to consummate the connection, I shuffled the pages, shifted them around, tried this, that, and the other position. But alas, it was to be no more than a series of futile knocks, one unanswered call after another, like someone crying out in the wilderness or searching in vain for home in the infinite void of outer space. When all was said and done, some sensitive yet crucial link, some delicate and subtle liaison was never established, and the pearly gates never opened for me.

No matter; we would try again. In my mind's eye I could see those exalted clerics and academics basking in the beautiful Provençal countryside, taking in a glorious sunset or lifting their voices in songs of praise, unencumbered by the toils and troubles that bedevil common people like us. With the echoes from their hosannas reverberating in my ears, I sank into an exhausted sleep. The heady bouquet of a good Bordeaux, the dazzling palette of the Impressionists — these things permeated my dreams as I drifted in and out, in and out of a fitful slumber.

My paper on literature and transcendence never did get faxed. Instead, on my machine, eventually a series of red lights began to flash, followed by a green light, then another red light. Worse, she started making all kinds of strange clucking noises. Finally she spewed out a puff of white smoke. Heavens, she'd come down with something!

I was completely distraught. The deadline was well past, but I still hoped to make it somehow. I really wanted to connect with that sublime transcendental world I so fervently believed in, to communicate my ideals and aspirations to others. At the same time, I felt very strongly that the most important task at hand was to take care of this earthly, earthbound fax machine. In her hour of need, there could be no doubt that my duty was to help her through her crisis and see that she recovered completely.

So I tried everything: I gave her massages and shiatsu treatments, fed her all kinds of mild paper purgatives, took her pulse and checked her heartbeat. To help her clean out her gastrointestinal system, I scooped up whatever sheets of paper were at hand and gave them to her for a diagnostic run-through. That was how a dissertation about transcendence came to be interleaved with directives on nutritional therapy and plumbing repair. When I took her pulse again, pressing gently against her acupoints, this hodgepodge of a composition went sailing through the machine. I had no idea where those incongruous pages would end up nor what the reactions of those who received them might be. Anyway, such things were not my concern. Caught as I was between transcendence and the fax machine, all I could do was to take care of the most urgent matters to the best of my ability, given the circumstances, and hope that somehow through all this I would be able to find a way out.

The Romance of the Rib

■ *Translated by Shirley Poon and Robert Neather*

He lost a rib in a car accident. It happened on the campus of the University of Chicago. He had gone there to participate in an international conference on cultural criticism, and had just given a presentation that afternoon, his discussion ranging from Habermas's notion of the 'public sphere' and Eagleton's *The Function of Criticism*, to the complicated and diversified cultural ecology of the small island he came from. From there he moved on to discuss certain 'public spheres' which had been created and still existed, and on to the limitations and possibilities of cultural criticism. Cultural scholars from different regions had expressed their various views, and a vigorous discussion had continued until well after the formal conclusion of the conference. An older friend was driving across the campus. The four of them in the car were planning to watch an old movie that was being shown on the campus that night. They were still exploring the topic of the afternoon's debate in the car, comparing the situations in the various Chinese communities around the world. It was a very lively discussion. Then suddenly the friend sitting in the front next to the driver suddenly yelled, 'Watch out!' He turned his head to look through the window. They were at a crossroads, and the bonnet of a bright red sports car came charging straight towards them from the left. Before he had a chance to react, the car had already collided with the door next to his seat. He felt a sharp pain in his left chest, opened his mouth, but was incapable of making any sound whatsoever. Everything went black before his eyes, and he passed out!

He had no idea how long he remained unconscious. In the end he couldn't tell whether he was still in the middle of a nightmare or whether he had actually woken up. He felt feeble all over, his head was spinning, the slightest movement brought back the pain and made him doubly aware of the heavy, stifling pressure in his chest. A fat, black woman doctor came in and told him in a pleasant enough tone of voice that a rib in his left chest had been broken into several pieces. They had given him first aid, then they had taken advantage of his coma to anaesthetize him and remove the bone fragments surgically. By now, the wound had gradually healed up. It was quite understandable that he should be feeling weak and dizzy. He had been comatose for two days, but now he was basically past the crisis. As long as he received proper nursing care, he would recover. She assured him that even with one rib missing he could still be a complete person. Just as she was about to leave, she even turned back jokingly and said to him, 'Do you want to have a look at your rib?' He was determined not to appear overly sentimental or narcissistic, and shook his head. 'Well, forget it then,' she went on. 'Anyway they can't remember whether they put it in room A03 or A04. I can't understand it. Apparently it just vanished! I still haven't managed to find it yet... Maybe God took it — to create a woman!' She winked, and went out laughing loudly. He wanted to force a smile, but the slightest pulling movement caused him a sharp pain in the chest. All he could do was clench his teeth, and close his eyes tight.

He had to be admitted to hospital again once he'd got back to the small island. He fainted suddenly as he was walking down the road. Even the doctors couldn't identify the origin of his condition. Their diagnosis was that he still hadn't made a full recovery, and that he needed time and rest in order to rebuild his strength. He lay there on his hospital bed, his mind wandering wildly, not really satisfied with this analysis. He had this strange feeling that ever since the car crash, his body had undergone a certain fundamental change. Maybe the missing rib on his left side had caused his body to lose its sense of balance. He even seemed to see things from a shifting perspective, more like a mirage than a normal perception of reality. Parallel and symmetrical compositions no longer seemed quite so neat and perfect. Rational thinking permeated his brain like a spider's web, but he just let it disperse. It was inadequate to deal with his current preoccupation. His thinking had been structured, as compact and tightly organized as the structure of a human skeleton. Now it was as if a gap had been opened somewhere, loosening the original order of things. He felt a huge hollow space in his chest, and a need to fill it with something new. On the plane home he had had a dream, in which the fat, black woman doctor had said to him, 'So you don't want your rib back? Then how can you hope to be your old original self again?' The next thing he saw was God standing behind her, saying to him, 'I used your rib to create a woman!' Then God disappeared too, and behind where God had been there appeared another woman, smiling sweetly at him. He felt something he had never felt before.

When he awoke, he struggled to remember the sweetly smiling woman's face, but with no success, no matter what he did. At the same time certain parts of the dream lingered in his mind, parts that made him feel ashamed, that seemed preposterous! It was simply a combination of clichés from popular fiction and elements of absurd superstition! What a waste of all the years he'd spent poring over the theories of the Frankfurt School, studying Adorno's critique of the popular cultural industry! After some minutes of futile self-reproach, he wandered in the region between sleep and wakefulness, trying to recapture that face.

The day he was due to leave hospital, he felt much better. He went to the cafeteria alone at lunch-time, and gorged himself on a dish of fried noodles with bitter gourd and beef. He felt as if he was returning to the human world for the first time after an absence of several years. He was seeing real human faces again. There was a girl sitting at the same table opposite him, tucking into a piece of barbecued spare ribs. On another table nearby, some nurses were chatting and laughing loudly. It was really not like a hospital at all — more like a school canteen! He wiped his mouth, took a sip of tea, and was about to get up, when he caught a glimpse of the girl's face opposite him — it was as if he had seen it somewhere before. He hesitated, felt a racing in his heart. He ordered another cup of coffee, and sat down again.

There was really no special reason for him to start fantasizing that this girl before his eyes was his rib. True, she was quite skinny, and when they first met she had been eating a dish of barbecued spare ribs — but that proved nothing! She looked familiar, but even he himself could not be certain she was the shadowy figure he had seen in his dream.

They started to talk very naturally. He thought the conversation was going rather well. Despite their different backgrounds, they had similar views on such things as the relative proportion of bone and meat in their meals, from which it could be deduced that they shared a similar outlook on life. He felt that in her he saw something of the sense of initiative and assertiveness of his younger self, a critical appraisal of meat *per se*, with a concurrent sympathy towards bones as matter. He was therefore almost inclined to believe that they *were* in some sense the missing parts of each other. Ever since a girl — a girl he had been more than a little fond of — had cheated him out of a hardcover set of the complete works of Marx, he had developed sceptical views on the subject of human relationships. He had already become accustomed to living a single life. But since the accident, his whole personality seemed to change. It drifted, floated loose. The sense of emptiness caused by the missing rib grew daily, and he longed to fill this emotional void. Now his unhappy memories of the past seemed to have gone, and in their place he found himself gradually developing a new line of communication with this new girl. She was a specialist nurse who came in to work every Friday, so he went back to the hospital to have lunch every week on that day, as naturally as if he'd been returning for regular check-ups or to collect a repeat prescription. He had started to feel uncertain about things, and there was no better remedy for this new sense of insecurity than a fixed time for lunch and a kind, cheerful friend. He felt that he had found a relatively simple solution for his complicated, confused life. It was as if, having experienced a prolonged transitional state of drifting, he had finally found an anchor. Every Friday when he saw her eating her barbecued spare ribs, this was what he wanted to ask her in his heart, these were the words he was never able to utter: 'Are you my rib?'

The accident changed him visibly, steering him away from his previous generalized concern for society and culture towards a much more individualized (and perhaps self-indulgent) mode of self-reflection. In an article for a cultural criticism journal he produced a densely argued analysis of his own missing rib, arguing that 'such anomalies of skeletal development' were not entirely the fault of society, and going on to provide an exhaustive catalogue of his own dreams and fantasies. This elicited some sarcastic remarks from one of the journal's editors, and a bright young scholar, in his maiden contribution to the journal in question, leapt into the fray, tearing him apart in a relentless critique. The strange thing was that his article simultaneously attracted the attention of the International Rib Association, which judged it to be the most innovative 'rib article' of the year, and invited him abroad to give a public lecture on the topic. He was more than happy to go and exchange information with specialists. But once he was there he was preoccupied with how much he was missing the girl who liked to eat barbecued spare ribs.

He found out that some of the International Rib specialists were quite amusing to meet, while others were a good deal less amusing than he'd anticipated. But at the end of the day, none of them could suggest an effective treatment for his symptoms. The majority were 'rib-centred' theorists. They were especially, indeed predominantly, interested in their own ribs. This lent their theoretical expositions a certain conservative solidity, while also imbuing it with an undeniably cliquey, elitist quality. They were the owners of full sets of ribs and proud of the fact. He thus became more than ever the person who lacked something, the incomplete one. Their completeness gave them a sense of self-satisfaction; whereas his own lack prevented him from arriving speedily at any generalized position of his own, indeed disbarred him from affirming anything on the basis of what he actually possessed, obliging him instead to appreciate merit from the perspective of the external world, a world *other* than himself, as seen by people *beyond* himself. In certain other, relatively marginal specialists — specialists in minority areas such as big bones, small bones, more bones or less bones — he sensed a certain resonance. But then there were specialists who went to the extreme of eliminating dualism altogether, suggesting that there was no such distinction as that between bone and meat, even going so far as to propose that ribs themselves were a complete illusion, words without substance. These arguments he likewise found difficult to accept.

He wrote to Barbecued Spare Ribs when he was away on his travels, and received a brief letter from her in reply. He reflected to himself on her many qualities — for example, her quick tongue; or how neatly and noiselessly she gnawed the meat off her bones. He thought of their times together, those beautiful Friday afternoons when each of them had a bone. His turbulent, swirling thoughts finally came to rest with the conclusion that somewhere, outside those places that language was capable of illuminating, there existed an immense region of silence which he could never fathom. Sometimes a residual part of his old critical faculty came back to haunt him: 'Have I perhaps considered everything too simplistically?' But then again, there was no need to think of everything in too complicatedly a fashion, he comforted himself. He was just longing to meet her again.

Another Friday came along, and he walked down the road to the hospital filled with complicated emotions. On returning again to the small island, he had read the public attacks on his 'rib' journal article. It had been damned as in poor taste, meretricious, slight, lacking any positive or convincing insights. The young fighter had wheeled out the great master Lu Xun as a counter-example. Another critic borrowed some of his statements and twisted them to his own purpose. He was accused of not knowing anything about Lyotard (only *they* knew about Lyotard). He caught a whiff of something unnatural in the air. He read in the newspapers about the floods in eastern China, about the signing of the contract for the construction of the new airport, the upward movement of the Hang Seng Index, the liquidation of the BCC bank. A series of disasters and conspiracies. The inside cultural pages were full of the accusations and rebuttals of various opposing cliques in the visual arts and drama worlds. Every time he went abroad he spoke up for the island's culture, but the moment he came back he always felt so disappointed and pessimistic. The 'public sphere', of course, offered possibilities for dialogue, but even there the air was thick with prejudice, evil machinations, incomplete truths, untruthful slanders. He thought that if ever he were to do a presentation on cultural criticism again, this time he would probably avoid making such free use of the notion of the 'public sphere'. In fact it was highly unlikely he would ever participate again in any such conference. That way he might avoid the risk of losing another rib and going to hospital. But then how would he meet her? All he ever thought of now was her. She and he had both grown up in this same very special space. He could never invent a myth about a rib for her!

They were both very happy to see each other again. They talked about various things quite naturally. In the midst of the conversation he suddenly felt a hollow, dull pain in his chest. He couldn't help blurting out the words: 'Rib…' She laughed, and pointed to a piece of paper stuck on the wall. He couldn't decide if it was a menu or a piece of childish graffiti. The only words he could decipher on the paper were 'barbecued spare ribs', 'Peking-style spare ribs', 'golden roasted spare ribs….' He repeated the word: 'Rib…' She turned over the newspaper lying in front of her on the table, and he found himself looking at a series of colourful pictures with captions: 'bone, a piece of bone, pig's bone, rib-cage, spare rib, two rows of ribs, crotch, rod, cudgel, strip, iced lolly, chicken leg, banana, hairy gourd, cigar…' He observed to himself that his vocabulary never transcended the repertoire of the common man. He might actually *mean* something different, but the veins of language empowered him to go so far and no further. He was incapable of going beyond language and creating a myth of another world. Even if he told a romantic myth, it might still quite possibly turn into something banal, something composed of vulgar words. He suddenly remembered that twice today in their conversation she had already said: 'Someone else said exactly that before!' It made no difference that *he meant* something totally different from what anyone else meant. But then he looked at the menus stuck all over the wall, like talismans, and he was ineluctably drawn to the conclusion that, even if the two of them wished to enter into some sort of private communication, they were obliged to work with the rigging of public discourse!

To their right there was a newly-bought television. As he was talking to her, he found that her eyes were continually drawn to the lively images on the screen. He turned around to look too, but all he could see was a lady swaying her body and passing through a hoop. It looked like an athletic competition.

He decided to make one more futile attempt to arouse her attention, to explain what kind of person he was. He stood up and extended his arms in a great circle, imitating the shape of a rib-cage, trying to spell out his story in actions that went beyond language. She giggled, and proceeded to walk through the moon-door of his rounded arms. On her way out she uttered one word: 'Goodbye'.

The next day, he went to the hospital again. This was the first time he had been there on a day other than a Friday. He ate his lunch very slowly, and sat there afterwards from three to five, smoking. Gradually his heart seemed to grow more tranquil. He looked down into the canteen from the second floor. The rows of long tables down below were like — the metaphor he chose was needless to say relevant to his recent superstition — they were like the two rows of a rib-cage. The table at which he and she had been sitting before, was precisely one of the ribs on the left. And now it was empty. If he went and sat there, would there be another person looking down from above, thinking that *he* was his missing rib? He looked around. This too was a 'public sphere'. As things stood, it was impossible to say whether among the people present there existed relationships such as those between nurse and patient, or between a pair of friends, or lovers. He could walk across and sit down among strangers, he could interrupt their conversation, but he would be just a bright red sports car crashing recklessly into another vehicle, damaging the order of things, of the greater whole. In public spheres, there should be more respect for others, a greater sense of self-discipline. As for any further affinity, was that possible? He thought of that last gesture of hers, that swaying of the hips as she passed through the hoop. Surely, if in that moment she had not been his rib from his past, she would not have been able to sway like that, to walk away like that? Perhaps now things had changed. Perhaps now she was imbued with the life of another man's rib. He gradually came to terms with the idea that in reality there was no such thing as who was whose rib. Sitting there he had a larger vision of the whole. Each and every individual existed on his or her own, while at the same time entering into relationships with others. He wanted no more dreams of God, or the black woman doctor either.

Would he ever meet another rib-girl? This archetype, this myth might develop into an aesthetic obsession. Let it go! He suddenly realized something: he had not rubbed the pain in his chest for a long time. He had grown accustomed to life with a missing rib.

The Dentists on the Avenida de la Revolución

■ *Translated by Brian Holton and Agnes Hung-chong Chan*

Drizzle started falling just as we turned into Avenida de la Revolución. I kept worrying about the donkeys: would the paint on their bodies wash off in the rain? I still remembered the first time I stepped on this broad street and looked up at the sign: Avenida de la Revolución. I couldn't help getting all serious, snapping out of my tourist cool, just as if we were on a pilgrimage to some military establishment or visiting some vertiginous monument. But the very next minute I relaxed. After all, I'm just a modern Chinese guy who gets nervous at the mention of the word 'revolution'. The garishly-painted donkey cart in front of us was canvassing business from the tourists who packed the street. Was that a donkey or a horse? They'd painted it. My companion told me. Just at that moment I didn't get it at all: it wasn't until he pointed to the stripes on the beast that I suddenly realized what he meant. The poor donkey dropped its head docilely while his master waved to us, asking us to have our photos taken on his festooned cart. At this end of the Avenida de la Revolución, there was a donkey cart at every intersection, at the head of a long line of souvenir shops and restaurants with eye-catching signboards: Margarita's Village, El Mesón Español, Melissa 'Curios', and so on, decorated with busts of men wearing sombreros, fully-caped Mexican bullfighters, glasses of Margarita rimmed with salt — all local specialities designed to attract customers. The street was bustling with American tourists carrying newly-bought coloured rugs under their arms, and holding large paper flowers or walking sticks in their hands.

It wasn't a weekend, so there weren't many tourists down from the US, but the guy watching over the donkey cart still greeted us enthusiastically. Following his finger, I glanced at the blankets on the cart, with their red, yellow, black and green stripes, and the straw hats painted with flowers, piled up on either side. In between, there were pictures of two nearly naked Indians; they may have been meant to be Aztec heroes, but they looked more like Apaches in a Western. On a red-on-white signboard up above the cart were the words TIJUANA '1984' MEXICO, a convenient reminder for anyone taking a photo of exactly when and where it had been taken. We smiled and shook our heads. The man didn't insist, probably observing that Carlos didn't look like a tourist. We moved on a bit further, and a woman peddling bracelets and necklaces latched onto us. Carlos gently stroked the silver bracelets around her arm and said 'no' in Spanish, adding that we were in a hurry and had some important business to see to. The woman smiled and went on her way. We rushed on down the street. It was true — this time I hadn't come as a tourist. We really did have important business. We had come to recover a Chinese girl who was somewhere in Mexico, destitute and lost.

No, it wasn't as serious as it sounded. 'It's no big deal,' Carlos had said to me on the phone. 'I'll go with you on Monday morning.' So we went to the University International Student Centre early in the morning to pick up an I-20 form from the secretary and drove to the border in Carlos's car. 'How come she forgot to take her student ID with her?' Carlos wondered aloud as our car headed south on Highway 805. But that was the whole point: Weiwei was precisely the kind of person to forget her ID. Maybe when she heard there was a new student card, she assumed she no longer needed the old one to get back into the States. This was exactly what she said when she asked for our help on the phone. But had she even taken her Chinese passport with her? Carlos asked. I nodded.

She's almost as absent-minded as you are! he said. Since around 1980, when more and more mainland students started coming to study at our college, we had begun to feel that the distance between us was actually not so great as we'd imagined it to be. We'd get together to make *jiaozi* dumplings, and though the students from Beijing and Taiwan might fold the wrappers or do the last pinch a bit differently, their ways of rolling out the dough and scooping the stuffing seemed to be basically the same. We ate the dumplings together, dipping them in a mixture of red vinegar and shredded ginger. In general we agreed that *The Second Handshake* and *Regret for the Past* were really bad movies, but we all got excited talking about *Life* and *The River with No Buoys*. Weiwei told us that during the old days in Peking University when good movies were shown, there were so many people packing the place that the chairs were crushed out of shape. But when they put on *In Agriculture, Learn from Dazhai*, you couldn't even drag people in by force to see it. We all laughed at that. We did have some things in common. Perhaps we were too young to have strongly held positions, so we could still talk openly to one another about our likes and dislikes.

We made fun (in a good-natured way) of the Beijing students and their nightly habit of calling at each others' homes. We laughed at Weiwei because she behaved like her grandmother: they both wore glasses to read novels and they both had a weakness for sweets. Weiwei also liked to eat fruit and have a glass of hot milk before going to bed. One night when she found that she hadn't got any milk, she improvised and heated ice-cream instead. We just laughed at her for her creativity; we liked her for not bothering about the small stuff, for doing whatever she felt like doing. Even her absentmindedness made her feel somehow closer. In this respect we were alike. We really were descended from the same stock.

After dessert, Huang (she was from Taiwan) would urge her husband to relate Weiwei's story of the stamps. We were already cheering him on at this point, and some of us immediately started fighting among ourselves to tell the story to our new friends. Weiwei just sat in the corner, with a wry smile on her face, as if it was nothing to do with her. The story went like this. The previous summer holiday, Weiwei's husband, who was a visiting scholar in Canada, came to visit her in the States. Their son (who was still in the Mainland) loved to collect stamps, so he bought lots of stamps and brought them with him as presents to send to the boy. But for some unknown reason they soaked the stamps first, then put them on the door of a white cabinet to dry. When they tried to remove them, they found that the stamps had stuck to the paint. They scrubbed and scraped the cabinet door, pressing hard on it all the while. Eventually the door simply couldn't take the pressure, and came crashing to the floor, hitting the wall on its way down. Houses in California are built with flimsy walls, so the result was a hole in the wall. Weiwei and her husband had to go out and buy plaster to make good the wall. By now we were already rocking with laughter at the story. Huang even took us to see the wall and the cabinet in Weiwei's apartment: the cabinet door was covered with scraps of stamps — some of them recognizable as the head of the Queen of England, some of them depicting rare South American animals. And there was still a deep indentation in the wall.

'We still couldn't fix it!' cried Weiwei, shaking her head. Then she went on talking nonsense, and the whole thing got utterly ridiculous and over the top. We started making up completely absurd stories about her. '*Whaaat* — nonsense you're talking!' she protested in her own defence, drawing out the word 'what' like an old lady.

After that someone told us the story of the tenor who lived next door, and then some of us talked about the devout Hindu who lived downstairs. Someone said the Hindu's wife had left and another woman just like her had moved in to take her place. Someone else said it was still the same wife, but that she had put on weight. Yet another person said the Hindu had murdered his wife, hidden her body in the sofa, and thrown the sofa away when the landlord refurnished the house.

When the subject of the sofa came up, Weiwei suddenly raised a finger and remembered that she had just seen a beautiful sofa near the garbage dump. 'Let's go and see if it suits Liu,' she suggested. This person called Liu had just moved into the graduate hall of residence, into a room Weiwei had found for him. All our furniture in the hall was collected from other people's junk, or handed down from students who had graduated. Weiwei became an expert in this area not long after she came here. She used to make a tour of inspection every day at dusk to look for still-usable furniture, and when she found anything, she'd tell any Chinese students who were in need. She was a veritable one-woman information centre. Whenever she bumped into a couple, she'd ask if they wanted to rent out a vacant room in their house, because such-and-such a female mainland student was due to arrive in a month. Or when someone was assigned a room in the hall but he or she had found somewhere else to live outside the University, she would tell another student who needed the room. Liu's accommodation was arranged this way too.

When Liu moved into his new apartment, taking with him the high-quality hi-fi he had bought when he first arrived in the States, his boxes of new books, the suits and silk shirts he'd brought all the way from Taipei. There was everything he needed in the living-room, except a sofa. He phoned Weiwei and asked if there was a furniture shop nearby, and she promised to get him a sofa. So now at her suggestion, we all went downstairs and made our way to the garbage-dump to have a proper look at the sofa. The covers were still clean, and there were no obvious signs of wear. Under the upholstery one of the horizontal planks was broken, which wasn't really much of a problem. So we all lifted it up, hauled it across the road and set off. When we got tired, we dumped it right down in the middle of the road and sat on it to cool off. Finally, after a good rest, set off again and carried it to Liu's place.

Liu looked a bit suspicious. He thought there might be bedbugs in the sofa. 'Oh, come on!' Weiwei sighed. It was as if a world of personal disappointment was contained in those three words.

Weiwei always knew where to go on campus to see free movies which were being shown, and where to get bargains. She had recently been to a junk shop and bought a fake leather handbag for a dollar. She regularly went to the dentist in Mexico. Right, Mexico: it was only half an hour by car from the University to the border, and it cost just a few dollars to have a tooth filled in Tijuana — a dozen times cheaper than in the States. That's the sort of thing Weiwei taught us after she came here. When she rang last night to say that they wouldn't allow her back across the border, she sounded a bit worried, but added casually: 'That's OK, I'll stay here and have all my teeth checked!'

We got off at the border. I originally thought that Carlos would drive the car straight across, but instead he stopped in a parking lot near the border, and we got off and walked from there. One of my Hong Kong friends once said with some regret, 'It's so unfair! We can waltz into Mexico with no documents at all. But when we cross back into America, we get the third degree!' At the barrier, cars carrying tourists back to the US from their Mexican holidays were lining up for inspection. Dark-skinned Mexican children were weaving around the cars peddling flowers and toys to tourists. We headed right, over a bridge and past a bus-station, till we reached a vacant lot where several ebony dolls were displayed in a corner to attract tourists. Some of them were wearing traditional Mexican dress, and others were local versions of ET. Ahead, on a bridge over a dried-up riverbed, an old woman was hawking blankets. Beyond the bridge, was a row of shops selling handicrafts and clothes. The tightly-clustered houses and shops ran all the way up to the hillside in the distance. It was all so different from the wide open Californian landscape.

'This place always reminds me of Shenzhen,' Carlos said gently, referring to the new Chinese city that has sprung up across the border from Hong Kong. In a way it's true. The two places are similar — but at the same time quite different. A friend of mine once said Tijuana reminded her of Macau. That's true too. Especially when compared to San Diego, Tijuana is maybe more like something out of the Asia we are so familiar with. When I first came here and saw the potholes in the roads, the broken railings, the snack hawkers packing the street, I really felt like I was back home. On Californian TV we are always presented with Tijuana as a place with not enough water or a devalued peso, a world utterly different from California. To American tourists, it's a paradise for bargain hunters, an exotic destination, alive with Mariachi music and Margaritas. What can we say to their tales of adventures in bars and discos: we just feel differently. We come to Mexico less in search of exotic adventure. On the contrary, in Mexico we feel strangely close to the country, we even feel close to the poverty and dirt.

But Carlos didn't like Tijuana. 'You should go to Mexico City, or Acapulco,' he said. He mentioned several other places with many-syllabled, resonant names. I was in his house at the time, eating a pot of pork rind he made specially for us. That's another thing Chinese and Mexicans have in common! They both eat pork rind! It was spicy and at the same time refreshingly sweet. Carlos is an excellent cook. Only Mexicans know how to eat chillies! That was another of his pronouncements. Not to be outdone by the locals, I picked up a chilli about the size of my little finger and chewed on it. My mouth caught fire, and the tears poured down my cheeks! We held slices of lemon between thumb and index finger, sipped from small glasses of tequila, sucked at the lemon, and licked the salt from the back of our hands, all the while listening to Carlos's description of his travels in China.

He hadn't been back in more than thirty years! He had been working on an irrigation project and staying in Lanzhou at that time. He didn't leave until 1952. How the years had flown by! When he went this time, he was excited, and at the same time not a little disappointed. First, he hadn't expected so many of his old colleagues to be still around, but all of them came to meet him! They had been through so much, but they seemed just the same, and he could still pretty much recognize them. He was happy that those turbulent days were over. His main concern now was that while many old problems were still unsolved, a lot of new ones had come along. Yes, China was changing, but right now there were so many things to worry about! The old revolutionary fanaticism was fading away, but the quest for material gain could also distort people's true nature.

'In which case, even the good things of the past will completely disappear!' Carlos talked about businessmen who broke contracts, bureaucratic delays, and the bungles made by middlemen. Carlos knew a certain amount about Chinese people. He seemed to have preserved some of the idealism he'd had when he went to China as a young man. He still believed that people should live together on equal and friendly terms. He believed in making things by hand. He now ran a small textile factory in Mexico City, designing his own patterns and collecting various kinds of plain, beautiful folk designs — the ones he liked best. But he was afraid these things would lose their beauty if they were contaminated: lovely things can be corrupted, by politics, or by commercialization.

Whenever we praised the rugs in Tijuana, he would answer that there were much better ones to be had in Mexico City. He said that when he was on his way back and passing through Shenzhen, he saw a luxury hotel that had been built on a vacant lot. The bookshops were flooded with popular Martial Arts novels. He didn't like Shenzhen, in much just the same way he didn't like Tijuana. We still wanted to convince him that, somewhere behind the transitional shabbiness of Shenzhen, there was also a certain magnificence to China.

Carlos asked the bearded immigration officer if a Chinese girl had been there the day before. She's long gone, the man answered. Where did she go? We left and headed for the long queue outside, searching for a Chinese face in the crowd of strangers.

We always wanted to hear more from Weiwei about the situation in China. But the stories she told were never the kind of thing other people expected to hear. When she was asked about how things had been in the Cultural Revolution, she would say: 'There were no classes at all! I went swimming every day.' She said there had been no one working in the school canteen, and that the newspaper editorials encouraged teenagers to revolt. She, as an ordinary person, had been totally bewildered by all the unpredictable changes.

When Huang brought up some of the horrific reports that had come out of China, she would say things like: 'Yes, I know there were such cases!' But she didn't go on. Occasionally, she would grumble: 'Those magazines of yours in Hong Kong, sometimes they exaggerate things.' Someone asked if she had seen people being beaten to death in school, and she answered, quite casually, that she had. Her story was that there were two hostile groups of high school graduates, and when a guy went to the building where the other group hung around, he got beaten to death. End of story.

At first I thought it was because she was so worldly-wise that she didn't go any deeper into things. But later I found that she wasn't worldly-wise at all. She was about our age, and not particularly experienced. Perhaps she worried that her words would lead outsiders to believe in a distorted version of Chinese reality. Or perhaps it was more than that. Perhaps sometimes when a person has really gone through a hard time, they may not want to exaggerate their own experiences.

But sometimes she did talk about herself. For example, when we heard that she'd got to know her husband during the Cultural Revolution, we clamoured to know how, from just going swimming together, they had gone on to become lovers. She wasn't in the least bit shy: 'there was not much to it. We went swimming every day, and then we walked out together.' Someone asked: 'With so many people around, how did you know he liked you?' 'I didn't know at first; but later on, I gradually realized there was always this guy staying late every day. So we just met up and went home together....' We all laughed.

Things like this can happen anywhere. Weiwei's story came as a bit of a surprise to us. Before coming to the States, we'd read all sorts of stories from Hong Kong and the Mainland, full of revolutionary or romantic feelings. Somehow I couldn't see her as one of the protagonists of those stories — I couldn't imagine her raising her fist and shouting edifying slogans. Not could I see her as a radical spokeswoman, protesting at the way society and the times had betrayed her generation. That wasn't the sort of person she was.

She would only have been an unimportant character in those stories, probably appearing for one or two lines only, if at all. Perhaps she would have been the stay-at-home elder sister taking care of her old grandma while the leading lady went to the seaside or joined the revolution. Or she would have been the intimate friend who listened to the leading lady when she felt obscurely upset and started pouring out her feelings, or the one who made all the arrangements for the leading lady's funeral after she had nobly sacrificed herself in the cause. Or perhaps she would have been the plain girl with the pigtail, who gave a glass of water to the leading lady when she felt thirsty during her speech — a speech delivered on her return to China, after having invented the atomic bomb in America and turned her back on the seductions of American imperialism.

Weiwei was one of those people who just got on with their life without publicity, unconvinced by the relentless tides of fashion, someone who tried to think things through for herself and keep on learning. She occupied an inconspicuous place in the crowd, but she was nonetheless real, a down-to-earth real person. She studied hard and lived a simple life, but she wasn't so hardworking or penny-pinching that she acted against her own nature. We should have been happy that in those days we had someone like her among us, in our community of overseas Chinese students. She didn't blindly worship western things, she just had a natural desire to explore other people's culture, a simple curiosity.

She was studying oceanography. We always met her when we went to watch the weekly free European movies on campus, or when we went to talks on literature. When we walked past the lawn outside the hall, we could see from a distance that she had moved a folding chair out to sit reading in the shade of the trees. We sometimes met her at the house of the couple she lived with, having her lunch (usually a mixture of hot soup and leftovers from the day before). As she ate she used to browse through the Unicorn Bookstore's programme of art films, asking us things like, 'Is that movie by the guy called Fellini any good?'

Once when I was ill, she made a pot of rice porridge and asked me to take it back home. It was too dark and too dangerous for a girl to wait for the no. 34 bus outside the College of Oceanography after her evening classes, and she found a boy going in the same direction to accompany her. We might meet her by chance in a flea market or at someone's garage sale, holding a wooden comb she'd bought for fifty cents. Or we might see her buying fuzzy gourds at Wo Tsi Cheung, the local Chinese store. We saw her cycling past the road that led to John Muir College. We often saw her in the serial section of the library, reading the fiction pages of the latest edition of *People's Literature* or *Beijing Literature and Art*. Sometimes she would borrow old magazines and bring them back to our hall to tell us stories from them.

She didn't like the so-called 'scar literature' which had become so popular in the past few years, but she did like most of more recent fiction. When we asked her why, she tried to explain: 'It seems to reflect the problems in our daily life better.' She also talked to us about some of these problems herself, in most cases taking her examples from friends' or relatives' real life experience, and hardly ever from vague ideas or general principles.

For example, she mentioned a Chinese friend of hers in China who was planning to get married. He was so exhausted from running around preparing for the recently-revived traditional rituals — the wedding banquet, the dowry — that in the end he was no longer sure whether he actually wanted to get married.

She was such a marvellous story-teller that sometimes when we were halfway through a story, we forgot whether the people she was talking about were fictional characters or her real-life friends. We gradually got to know them: the young guy who finally applied for transfer to Shanghai but couldn't find a job there; the housewife busy all day with her job and the housework whose husband wouldn't lend a hand, who'd given up her dreams but went on making up fairy tales for her children; the unknown artist who made carvings which only he liked; those three poverty-stricken friends who all got together at the end of the year to help each other out; the young girl who rejected the prevailing commercial mood of her town; the optimistic, enthusiastic old revolutionary and the young modern girl he met, who was sceptical, disappointed and suicidal.

These characters were relatively realistic and approachable. When we were discussing some film we'd seen, and commented that the woman coming to study in the States was unreal and unbelievable, Weiwei drew us pictures of other characters.

In one of her favourite stories, an ordinary forester, who had worked away unheeded all his life, came back from a visit to his relatives in the States and was at once blown up by the press into a patriotic intellectual who had refused a handsome legacy. This greatly bewildered him. 'This man, Liu Chi,' said Weiwei, 'was no different to millions of foresters toiling away like ants all their lives, except for two things: his grandfather had killed somebody, and his aunt was an American resident. It made sense to praise him for his tree specimens, for his notes, or for his general love of trees and forests, or his love of his homeland, but it was really silly to glorify him on the grounds that he'd been cold-shouldered by his American aunt!'

Weiwei had relatives in San Francisco too. Before visiting them at Christmas, she went to Tijuana and bought lots of gifts for their kids. She really loved Tijuana. 'Things are cheap and unusual there——the best gifts for kids!'

She went to San Francisco with her husband and had a great time there. Her husband bought a camera and he saw everything through the camera lens — the landscape, the city landmarks. 'It's all so beautiful!' he cried. She narrowed one eye, copying him, as viewed the world through the window of his new toy.

They also bought presents to send to their son in China. Did the boy ever spare them a thought? He was hard-hearted little fellow. On a tape he mailed them, he said he didn't think of them in the least, in fact he said that he had almost forgotten them. This made the old grandparents back in China feel so bad, they recorded a few words later on, saying that this wasn't true.

Weiwei was paying her own way, so she definitely had to return to China when she finished her studies. Not because she was a 'patriotic intellectual', or anything like that, but because she hadn't thought of an alternative. She only shook her head in disapproval at the students whose main concern was to succeed in taking back with them to China their precious quota of 'eight big white goods' (washing-machine, fridge, computer, etc), or else to get hold of quotas from other people to use themselves.

She was like one of those characters in her favourite modern stories: not particularly smart by the usual standards, and yet finding joy in her own way. She didn't want her natural feelings to be distorted by material considerations. She just wanted to be an absolute nonentity, sunbathing and reading the latest news magazines to keep up with whatever was happening in the world. Like her old grandma, she would get up during the course of a sleepless night, touch this and that object in the house, have a cup of coffee, read a short story, or write a long letter. Once she was talking about how tall her son was, and added that she was quite small herself because she was born prematurely. That was why her parents called her 'Weiwei' — Little One.

It wasn't going to be easy to spot such a plain, tiny figure in the confused riot of colours along the Avenida de la Revolución. We looked on both sides of the street, sometimes turning into Calle Zapata or Calle Diaz, or walking along the Avenida de la Constitución which ran parallel to the Avenida de la Revolución. Carlos went to several dental clinics he knew. The patients in the waiting room looked up. A young guy behind the counter flipped through the register. A wide-eyed nurse shook her head with a smile. They all gave the same answer: 'No, no.' One white-robed dentist, a small, thin, middle-aged man with an ordinary face, came out to chat with his patients. They were like passengers bumping into each other on a bus.

We went down some steps and walked past a hawker selling *camarones* and a variety of other delicacies on the roadside. Then we stopped in front of a coconut stall. We bought a coconut, halved it and shared the sweet, refreshing milk. Then we cut out two slices of white coconut flesh and chewed them. The morning drizzle had long stopped, and the sun was shining weakly. There seemed to be light flowing down the street, casting a series of reflections on drenched surfaces, mottling the white walls. The fresh morning air smelled like coconut.

At the side of the street, there was a stall selling tortillas. A stout woman turned the tortillas over with her chubby hands. They looked delicious. You can find people baking tortillas everywhere in Tijuana. Their stoves vary in size, the tortillas may be more or less burnt, and they fill them with all sorts of different things — chillies, tomatoes, carrots, meat. No matter. This is what everyone eats. On the street, people talked loudly with one another, walked past, stopped to buy or haggle. It was just a perfectly normal scene from daily life. We could have been on a street in China, as we gazed around us, looking into every face in the search for our missing person.

Sometimes there were moments when we seemed to forget what the person we were looking for actually looked like. At those moments, if we reflected on it, it was as if we hardly knew her very well at all. After all, we came from two such different societies, and held such different views on certain things. When we met for the Book Club, for example, and read stories written in Hong Kong or Taiwan, sometimes Weiwei couldn't understand why these authors were so interested in writing about topics which to her seemed so insignificant. Whereas we saw things differently: China was undergoing fundamental changes, and perhaps these changes affected (and changed) the very notion of what issues were worth writing about and how they should be written about. Perhaps in a modernized society, people would consider different issues important?

Weiwei also said that she couldn't understand Liu: he decorated his apartment with exquisite taste, he bought his girlfriend perfume, cosmetics, funny toys and the best jewellery. They lived together, and then broke up after less than two months. How had things turned out in this way? All sorts of incomprehensible ways of behaving in this new world around her puzzled Weiwei, and made her ask questions. When we went around to her house to borrow her vacuum cleaner, there were several Beijing students who had dropped in too. She asked us to stay and have some fruit. She told us she wanted to save money for a trip back to China after sitting her exam next year, and wondered whether she would be allowed to bring her son to America for a short vacation. Just then the phone rang. It was Liu. He said his girlfriend was leaving, and he wanted to move to a smaller apartment. He entrusted Weiwei again with the task of asking around and finding him a suitable place. So Weiwei asked us to help him out.

The students from Beijing were all studying science. But they all watched new films by directors like Francis Coppola and even started listening to modern music. One of them wore his hair much longer than when he first arrived. They occasionally dropped hints that perhaps Weiwei was having problems with her husband, even implying that she might want to stay on in America. But so far as I could see, there was no sign of her having made any such decision. I dare say I saw things differently, and the Weiwei I perceived was different from theirs. But in any case we were all young and optimistic, and got along well, even though our views on many topics were quite far apart.

Once one of our group of students praised a photo taken by David Hamilton, which led us on to a discussion of the aesthetics of commercial photography. I found myself thinking of some of the particularly lurid magazines that had recently started appearing in Guangzhou, reprinting juicy gossip from the Hong Kong showbiz world. We found such stuff stale, but a writer from the Mainland thought this phenomenon reflected some sort of openness (on the part of China). We were coming from such different spaces. They had experienced the extreme leftist line of thought during the Cultural Revolution, and saw the current trend toward commercialization as a means of striving for freedom and openness. They were most reluctant to see their new and hard-won freedom of speech restricted as a consequence of a clamp-down on commercialization. By contrast, we had grown up in a commercialized society, and were fed up with the plausible lies perpetrated by advertising and the media in general. Besides, in our society the mainstream mentality, of which commercial marketing was merely one symptom, very much dominated the general mindset, and suppressed other non-mainstream and more creative ways of thinking. But our mainland friends hadn't experienced this, and so they weren't able to understand our point of view.

On another occasion, when we were talking about the funding of our graduate school and its research policies, they found themselves supporting the US policy which allowed the Department of Defense to allocate funds for research in graduate institutes, thus giving those institutes a lot of resources with which to buy equipment and employ people to do research. But we thought this was precisely where the problem lay: the Reagan administration's practice of linking education and defence created a situation in which academic research served government policy, which in turn destroyed the reflective, independent and critical function of scientific research, and so reduced it to a political tool. They were painfully aware of the poverty of their own universities back in China, the lack of facilities and funds, and they couldn't help envying the affluence they saw around them. Again, we were coming from different spaces, we saw things differently.

They were looking forward to the benefits of increased consumption and production, while we on the contrary saw all of the disadvantages of commercialization. We often saw Weiwei sitting by herself with her head bowed, as if she was deep in thought, pondering the fate of her country, and the changes it was going through.

We walked down the alleys, past the stalls. I looked at the mass-produced handicrafts on sale, many of which had been made to look like Mickey Mouse or some Extra-terrestrial, something to conform to the tastes of American tourists. I recollected that the last time I had been in Carlos's house, he had gone so far as to say that it was no longer possible to buy real Mexican handicrafts in Tijuana. I wasn't quite convinced, not until he showed me the things in his house. What a wonderful, varied, colourful world, so full of vitality, so vividly imagined! These were not fancy accessories and baubles, but the ordinary clothes and articles of daily life, handmade and still in everyday use. They were in the shape of everyday objects, fruits, plants and animals, and painted in bright, fantastic colours: a teacup with a human face, a crouching crocodile-like stool made of coloured beads, a bottle gourd painted with scenes from stories, fish and bird tapestries, a mermaid boat, a Tree of Life candlestick, and a shallow incense-burning bowl with crawling pygmies. Shoes, clogs, wallets, shirts, furniture, cups and pots, rugs, tables and chairs, baskets, and musical instruments. The images of creatures on these handicrafts were quite simple and without much detail, and yet they exhibited a kind of childlike clumsiness which was beautiful. They seemed like a physical embodiment of folk wisdom and imagination. Those were Carlos' words.

I drew a parallel between these crafts and Chinese folk art. The Shaanxi cloth toys and cloth articles for daily use, the traditional embroidered stomachers, and traditional cummerbunds also had that quality of being at the same time lively and simple. During this evening in his house, Carlos said that during his recent trip to China, he had seen people in the open market selling photos of Hong Kong and Taiwan movie and TV stars, sportswear with American slang expressions printed on it, and even gilded plastic images of Buddha and the Virgin Mary.

I recollected the Guangzhou I had seen in 1973, towards the end of the campaign to criticize Chairman Mao's former 'comrade-in-arms' leader Lin Biao and the ancient sage Confucius. Slogans everywhere. I had seen threadbare lengths of white cloth inscribed with great blood-red characters hanging in front of a restaurant, while inside the customers bent over their food in miserable silence, the walls above them pasted with more slogans.

Since then, more than a dozen years had passed and great changes had taken place. What path would China take now? What did the future hold? Carlos also asked these questions. He was not being in the least satirical. He insisted that despite everything, he had still encountered many honest individuals on his recent trip, men who kept their promises. Many of his old friends hadn't changed. You could still meet with some sincere person here and there, a human being who glowed with genuine beauty, like a creature made of simple clay. Anyway, perhaps we should carry on along this bustling, seedy street, continue our search among the crowds of ordinary people. Suddenly Carlos caught sight of something at the far end of the avenue. '*Qué muchacha china bonita!*' he cried out. Following the direction of his finger, I saw her, the 'lovely Chinese girl', sitting on a roadside bench behind a rank of messy stalls. It was Weiwei! She looked quite lost, sitting there with a vacant look, perhaps listening to the noisily haggling crowd. Or perhaps she had settled herself down to one side so as to think about her own problems.

The morning sunlight cast mottled shadows on her body. The pigeons flew past her. And yet she noticed none of it. Perhaps she hadn't slept well the night before, or perhaps she was a bit tired after a long walk along the street. Or perhaps she just wanted to sit there and think, before standing up and continuing on her way again.

Postcards from Prague

■ *Translated by Tong Man, Jasmine*

1.

Dear Hannah,

I've arrived in Prague and it's the evening of the day of Havel's inauguration, and even though I'm just passing through I can feel the excitement in the air. It'll take place in St. George's Basilica. An old man said to me excitedly, 'They're using the old ceremony for the first time in 50 years.'

After I settled down I went to look for that toy salesman at the address I've got for him. The houses of the city look quite old, but for some reason familiar. Passing through the square, walking around in the cobbled streets and looking at the elegant old palace, I can't help thinking about all those years ago when Beethoven or Mozart came here looking for rich patrons. Did they walk along the same road? Looking at those simple, almost crude, old houses and those winding little alleys, I think about Kafka — I first read him when I was a teenager — and think about looking for a way out of this maze. I laugh at myself. How come I've become such a romantic these days? Maybe it's because I'm thinking about you, Hannah. If you were here, you'd definitely love this place. But, as a middle-aged toy salesman passing through Prague with my suitcase, all I want to do is to find out about the products and the market here, to see if there's any business after the change.

I got some information and I've made an appointment to visit the toy factory tomorrow. I haven't forgotten the toy you want me to find for you — the A630287 model, the paper garden. But the shopkeeper said they haven't produced any since '68. Then he said he would ask another factory and see if they have any in stock. I've copied down several addresses of old toyshops and I'll go and have a look in the next few days. Oops! I've written too much and there's no space left.

Take care,
Lee Ping

2.

Dear Hannah,

I just sent the first postcard. Watching it drop into the letter-box covered with such closely written characters I couldn't help laughing at myself. So now, just as a joke at my own expense, I'm going to send you another.

Because you collect postcards, I promised to send you some before I left. Actually I'm not at all the kind of person to send postcards. Postcard-writing should be concise, humorous — a few incisive witty remarks, a few open secrets of a personal nature, a suitable degree of familiarity, some explanation of the picture on the other side, a bit of harmless teasing. More suited for people who know where to draw the line, who can do free skating in their postcard writing. But everything I do is always over the top. Like the last postcard I wrote — too long, just like the first half of a letter. I even used up most of the space for the address. See! I'm no good at this game.

I'm having dinner in this open-air café, sipping chilled white wine and eating smoked oysters as an appetizer. But Havel's broadcast on the radio has caught my attention. Nearby there's a pair of lovers who never stop kissing, even while they're busy translating the broadcast for me. Maybe because Havel's words arrive through those kissing lips, I can feel particularly strongly his real humanity. He's so self-aware and humble in his hopes. I raise my glass to them again and again, for their country, for the emotions that those words arouse in me (even in translation).

Oh dear! I've gone on too long again.

Lee Ping

3.

Dear Hannah,

Prague is really a beautiful city. Here's another postcard for your collection. I spent the whole morning visiting the city. Now things have changed, the market here has quite a lot of potential. I've been thinking about a partnership with a toy sales company here. This afternoon I went to those old toyshops on the addresses I copied. I wanted to find you the toy but had no luck.

Wandering around the city I dropped in at a bookshop. They had a book by the author you mentioned but it was printed in an alphabet neither of us can read. I knew if I just bought the book with the name and the photograph printed on it you'd be very excited when you saw it. So I picked it up — it was quite thick — and went to the cashier and then I thought how silly it'd be to buy it, so I put it back.

I've still got one last address. Apparently it belongs to the oldest toyshop in town. I hope I can get you the toy tomorrow.

Lee Ping

4.

Dear Hannah,

Across the river, away from Charles Bridge and the Castle and away from the crowds of tourists, in a narrow alley in the old district, I found that old toyshop. The shopkeeper is an old man with silver hair and a silver beard, like a character in a fairy tale. The first question he asked was 'Do you enjoy making models yourself?'

I was sorry to disappoint him. I'm not much of a businessman, and I certainly can't pretend to be young and innocent enough to be a model-maker. So I said, 'No, it's for a friend of mine, a girl who's twenty years younger than me.'

He went up into the loft for quite a while and came back down covered in dust. 'I really haven't got one,' he said. 'In fact it's a long time since I last had one.' I was disappointed, but I thanked him anyway. Before I left he said 'Excuse me, Mr. Chinaman. When you go back, will you ask your friend why she asked you to come all this way to find a model of a beautiful Chinese garden?'

I sat and had a drink in the open air café halfway up the hill again. This is my last night in Prague. There's a bit of a problem with the partnership. I've had second thoughts about it. Something's come up that I hadn't expected and can't sort out right now. I don't want to tell you the details. Maybe they're not quite the thing for your young mind.

I drank glass after glass looking at the lights at the bottom of the hill and somehow for no reason at all, I thought about you. You might wonder why I should think about you in these circumstances: for no particular reason, just because I'm missing you, thinking about you, thinking about all that you represent. I've written too much again. I don't know whether I'm going to post this or not.

Greetings from a man who doesn't really like writing postcards and who's trying to send you a postcard on his last night in Prague.

Lee Ping

Borders

■ *Translated by Shuang Shen*

Less than half an hour after the performance was over, everyone had left. My friend had said he might drive down from New York, but failed to show up, and I found myself alone on the square outside the theatre, the lights behind me going out one by one, the trees and bushes all around slowly melting into ominous pools of shadow. I finally awoke as if from a dream and grasped the seriousness of my situation. I'd never find a bus back over the border to Washington DC at this hour… There was no hope of finding a bed for the night, or of being taken in by some kind stranger. I was genuinely down and out! I'd gone too far again, strayed too deep into alien territory, landed myself in trouble — and all for the sake of some obscure new show.

If I close my eyes, I can still see the sorry picture I must have presented that night, scrambling pathetically after tail-lights as cars flashed past into the darkness, searching helplessly for a security guard or a public telephone, knocking on doors to no avail. The night grew colder and colder, until finally I realized that this was it, it was really happening, this was the sort of disaster I'd never once experienced during all my ten years of backpacking in the 70s. If I'd been a local I'd have been snugly in bed and asleep by now. If I'd been a well-organized tourist I'd have made careful plans ahead of time. But I'm neither. I'm a wanderer by nature. I enjoy crossing borders, I take a perverse pride in it. Which is why I so often end up alone like this, a roaming ghost, orphaned and without a home.

Now that it's over I can see that this experience probably had some symbolic significance, which is why I am writing it down and telling you the story now. But at the same time, I've gradually come to realize that all recollection of the past is an exercise in futility. How am I really supposed to tell the story of that trip of mine to Washington DC? Or of any trip, come to that? When I came back to Hong Kong in 1983, I began telling stories about Paris. In 1990 I had a chance to stay in Berlin and spent my entire time there writing a story about Hong Kong. I wrote about Berlin while I was in New York, and about New York in Washington DC. Now here I am back in Hong Kong, wanting to write about Washington DC. Stories of the past never catch up with the ever vanishing present. The present constantly alters memory — which is why the quest for the past is such a futile exercise. I used to believe everything could be accounted for, everything could be consigned to its proper place in time and space. Later I discovered this to be an illusion. And yet, yes, history does stick together, somehow or other. The past coheres, in its own fashion. And all we can do is speak to the present from its interstices.

Should I, for example, focus on the shaking paper cup and the spilt coffee on the train? Or the fax in my pocket, the one that had arrived earlier in the day, and had made me miss a previous train? Or should I be altogether more objective and matter-of-fact? 'December 1991, here I am in Washington DC. Impressive skyscrapers. Distant view of the White House. Walked past the Vietnam War Memorial. Got lost trying to find Spalding Gray's one-man show.'

Where should I stand in the sculpture garden — in the centre or on the periphery? Should I sit cradled in the arms of a giant statue? Or should I watch from the edge, next to one of the sculpted human figures up against the wall? That's it. I'm searching for a perspective, wondering who I'm writing for, and why, and whether there's any meaning to it. If I write about Washington, or Berlin, or Shenzhen, maybe I can't recollect those journeys as they occurred, but as I crawl across the page, the words themselves become a journey. And then there's the distance between us, between you and me, which has varied with time. I don't know if I can ever transcend that distance, I don't know if somehow one day I can cross that border.

I'd like to start by telling you about my search for Gray's one-man show. The natural starting point for anyone writing about Washington is of course the Library of Congress, or to be more precise on this occasion, the exhibition of maps they had on at the time. Needless to say, all old American maps revolve around Washington. It was and is the centre. But I was there to see Gray's show. That was my centre... Someone had told me he was giving a show at George Mason University, a show called 'A Personal History of American Drama'. I was curious to see what sort of connection he was going to make between personal history on the one hand and American drama on the other. But no one seemed to know where George Mason University was. The maps certainly told me nothing. All the old maps in the exhibition, no matter how they were drawn, placed Washington in the centre. Perhaps that's the way capitals always are — with their spotless subways, solemn grey stone walls, and grand architecture. The meaning of every part of the world is defined in terms of distance from capitals. On the old maps, the further a place is from this important centre, the more 'desolate' it is supposed to be. By extension, a university that doesn't feature on the map at all is a university that quite simply doesn't exist. And therefore, the show I had come all this way to watch must equally be a non-existent show ...

'Lolita, while I was packing this morning the owner of the Lebanese store on Fourteenth Street called to tell me there was a one-page fax waiting for me I want to reply to your fax before I board the train for Washington Don't go rushing into a decision about whether to apply to a university in the US. A more positive way of using this period of time would be to make yourself better prepared and try to get to know Hong Kong better I don't know why you keep saying there's nothing good about Hong Kong Maybe

I'm just odd Why do you keep trying to be someone else… I'm sorry to pour cold water on all your plans and bring you down like this just when you're feeling so happy but I don't think escaping to the West will solve the emotional problems you're having right now.'

'Ah Bei, last time you asked me how I rate the one-man shows in Hong Kong. I've been thinking about it. When I got to New York, I made a point of watching a few one-man shows, and I went to see "Sex, Drugs, Rock & Roll", the film adapted from Eric Bogosian's off-Broadway performance. I also went to see Laurie Anderson, and a film based on some of Gray's live material. Eric Bogosian puts on other people's "faces" so as to portray a gallery of various personalities, from Wall Street to the subway. Laurie Anderson's sensitivity to music and visual images allows her to explore new horizons through a combination of language and performance. Gray's autobiographical narrative has a style of its own. You said that some people want to put Chinese stand-up comics and joke-telling in this context. In a way these things *are* comparable, but a real one-man show is a genuine form of verbal art all of its own. It's not just a matter of making people laugh. It's full of all sorts of clever twists and turns and transformations.

'I'm in Washington for a conference. I've heard that Gray's giving a performance tomorrow, but still haven't managed to find out where. Tonight I went to see that old play "Fever", with Wallace Shawn (the fat guy in "My Dinner with André"). It used to be considered controversial. The way I see it, the piece uses the extreme sensitivity of the main character as a vehicle to expose the general psychological desensitization of modern man. It's very existentialist. Actually the long monologues in it are very like a one-man show.

'Last time you mentioned a debate you'd had with your friends around the issue of social relevance and one-man shows. The way I see it, a one-man show can start out as a personal monologue and then go off in several different directions. It can examine the psychology of an individual. It can make social comment. It all depends how deep the monologue-artist wants to dig. Gray's current show, "A Personal History of American Drama", sounds like it's going to be an attempt to link the personal with the historical. I've no idea if it will be successful. I don't even know if I'll be able to find the theatre. Will let you know if I ever get there.'

The most interesting thing about the monologue as a genre is its way of addressing the audience. It doesn't set out to lecture, to give an explanation of anything, to make some sort of personal statement, or to present some sort of self-analysis. It just grows and expands, it flows continuously and naturally. Gray came onto the stage with a bottle of water in one hand and just stood there and started talking non-stop. He talked about the 70s, how much he'd always wanted to join Richard Schechner's experimental theatre group, how lucky he was to have played the role of Macduff in 'Macbeth' as an understudy, and how by applying Schechner's new method in that production he'd learned to experience within his own body the limits of physical endurance, to internalize the cathartic power of blood and violence. Gray referred to the madness of his time with the theatre group, when it was in residence. It all began with some incident involving a stolen piece of barbecued beef and then developed into total hysteria and chaos.

But he himself never ate the meat. Or so he said. Strange. In a way his monologue seemed to take us all back to the strange passions of a bygone era, and yet his language indicated that he'd left the crazy 70s behind, put a certain distance between that era and himself. Some monologues tend to be long-winded and boring, others are simply wonderful, novel and constantly intriguing. A monologue can be spontaneous and free-flowing like jazz, at times tight and intense, at other times more relaxed and laid-back. The trouble starts the moment we write anything down on paper. That's when words stick together so easily, when they fall into old set forms, into constantly repeated clichés. We want to break them up, these linguistic formulae, these thought patterns we have formed out of habit or laziness — but how? How can we keep on improvising and succeed in drawing out new feelings? These are the questions…

The exact same words can sound fresh or stale on different occasions. With repetition, the very same sentence can lose its life-force. I sit there in the audience waiting, never quite knowing what to expect from one minute to the next. I find myself thinking about a recent performance I went to see, of a play called 'Futz' at the La MaMa Theatre in New York. 'Futz' was a big hit thirty years ago. Everyone said what an important play it was at the time, but I'm afraid I couldn't identify with it. It's all about this man called Futz who falls in love with a pig, and about his ex-girlfriend Marjorie, and crazy Oscar who throttles *his* date (Ann) because he sees Futz having sex with the pig. In the end Oscar is sentenced to be strangled to death, and Futz is killed by Marjorie's older brother. The violence of the piece recalled something of the power of 60s and 70s theatre (Gray talks about that), but at the same time I couldn't help feeling that the simplicity and romanticism of 60s and 70s art, while it may have succeeded in liberating us from certain conceptual dead-ends, merely landed us in others, other simplistic modes of thinking, such as the unconditional worship of brute primitive force. The play's formalistic stage style seems so artificial and contrived now, for example the chant-like chorus. I feel I've moved a huge distance away from that kind of thing. I've seen a lot of new, creative drama in New York. I heard that the legendary Living Theatre were putting on a new play called 'Zero', and managed to find out their address. I'd read so much about them in the 60s and 70s, but this new play came as such a disappointment.

Gray talks about his mother's suicide. She killed herself because she couldn't cope with reality. Clearly it came as a devastating blow to Gray. What words, what kind of language, what devices can we employ to describe the process of surviving trauma? Is a single individual's depression connected to the whole sense of loss of a particular epoch? Do you think it makes any sense to set out from a subject such as American drama and move on to talk about one's own personal life? I now realize that the title of this show, 'A Personal History of American Drama', actually refers to *his* personal experience in the theatre, not to some vague personal history of his as seen from the point of view of American drama. It's the sort of piece that was bound to end up in the Black Box Theatre of a 'fringe' university located somewhere outside Washington DC, not on the main stage of the Kennedy

Center. In it he reconstructs, through free-flowing word improvisation, his own personal experience and his own sense of selfhood.

This self, this eclectic and ever-changing kaleidoscope, *is* connected in an infinite number of ways with the universe around it, and inevitably this web of connections becomes manifest in the monologue itself, as it evolves. Every turn in the monologue, every sentence, every new choice of words, ultimately heightens the tone and colour of the self-portrayal. He speaks about having once forgotten the address of a friend's home where he was staying. He vaguely remembered the shape of the keyhole, so when he wanted to go back there, he had to wander from door to door inspecting the keyholes of people's houses. Everyone laughs at this. Taking a sip of water, he adds: 'Of course, I've exaggerated certain details.' I like the way he deconstructs his own myth of self. I don't care whether his monologues make people laugh, or whether they have the slightest social significance — Ah Bei, what interests me is the way he explores and constructs these multiple selves in the fluid movement of his language. Some of his linguistic manoeuvres are subtle, others more obvious. Truth and fiction both play a part in it. In the end the subject of the monologue is not some significant incident or inspiring passion. It is the shape and potentiality of language itself.

Sometimes he begins a new subject only to stray away from it, and I find myself worrying that he has gone too far and will never be able to get back to his starting point. Other times his monologue moves ahead so fast I'm worried he won't be able to catch up with himself at all. But most of his fans, who have come all the way to this theatre at George Mason University, seem to appreciate and respect his way of doing things, his ways of moving through language, sometimes doing a somersault and landing a hundred miles away. When I asked around in New York and Washington, I was told that George Mason University didn't exist. I couldn't find it on any map of Washington, and eventually got the address from a recorded telephone message. By then I had already left Washington DC and was over the border, in the state of Virginia. How was I ever going to get back that night? It was no use worrying about it, and I decided to wait till the show was over. So I'd begun by searching for my destination on a map of Washington DC, and ended up straying somewhere off the map altogether.

I finally got off the bus and found the campus, but I still had trouble finding the Black Box Theatre. First I lost my way in a wood, and later, after the show, I wandered around the campus in the middle of the night, unable to find any form of transportation, I couldn't help asking myself several questions. Why am I always getting myself into trouble? Why do I have this constant desire to see more of life? Why do I keep wandering off the map, beyond my familiar territory, on some nameless quest? Why do I constantly place myself in situations of such insecurity?

'L — when I got to New York, I went to see your relations...'

I'm holding my pen in my hand, but can't think how to continue.

I've written a lot of letters to L in the course of the past few years. When I went to Berlin in the early 1990s, I took the subway to Friedrichstrasse Station and walked around the streets, trying to imagine what East Berlin once looked like. At the end of the day I sat down in a bar and started writing a postcard to L, excitedly describing everything I'd seen. Many of us had been so disillusioned by Tiananmen and what had happened in China the year before, we had transferred all our hopes to Eastern Europe. When we crossed the border to see the aftermath of the collapse of the Wall, we were all searching for something, some evidence to bolster our own sense of optimism for the future. The day after I sent my postcard, I saw a load of newly produced underground pornography in the bookshops, I heard people complain about unemployment, inflation, and the influx of Western culture. My West Berliner host stole a plaque from Marx-Engels Platz as a trophy to hang in his living-room. West German Yuppies were making a racket day and night, mocking their impoverished relatives from the East. Potsdam Platz, a wasteland for decades, was ripe for redevelopment. Huge Mercedes-Benz hoardings were about to go up.

'L — we seem to have written to each other quite frequently over these past few years, especially when we've both been travelling. I remember the first time we both went back to the mainland in 1973, how nervous we were as we walked past the border patrol at Lowu, and the armed PLA soldiers looked sceptically at our entry permits, where we'd put down 'tourism' as the purpose of our visit. We were coming to terms with our own marginality for the first time. Our re-arrival in Canton, a city which should have been so familiar and yet seemed so strange, started us thinking about a host of different things. I went off to see the Seven Star Rock in Zhaoqing, while you met a middle-aged man on the Wuzhou ferry, who reminded you of a character in one of Shen Congwen's stories. Then you got married, and you went to visit Guilin, and later you went back on several trips to other parts of the mainland. You wanted to stay close to China.

'I remember writing to you about my trips to Taiwan and Japan, about my life as a student in the US. When I was in Paris with D and Y at the end of 1982, I sent you a postcard, hoping we could meet up again when I got back.

'But when I did come back, I found you unwell, suffering from insomnia. Apparently you'd had a nervous breakdown. You said it was because your boss had changed your work shift, moving you from the 6.30 evening news to some early morning programme, which meant you had to get up at 3 or 4 in the morning and then couldn't get any sleep during the day. You'd started taking sleeping pills and drinking heavily. As we sat there chatting in the coffee house, I could see your hand shaking violently, and I insisted on taking you to see first a doctor, then a psychiatrist.'

Later I learned a bit more about what was going on, from a friend. It was a man called Wong, who'd been promoted to head the News Division, and had removed a whole group of older people from their positions. My friend L had been editor-in-chief of the Chinese News Division. Wong made a big thing of befriending him at first and then a few days later advised him to improve his career prospects by taking evening classes in journalism at Baptist College. Then, as soon as he had enrolled, Wong told him it would be easier for him to study if he did a morning shift. And so he was taken off his original evening news hour.

'When I went to the hospital to visit you, you were incapable of explaining your condition coherently. It was so sad seeing you in your white hospital pyjamas. I'd brought you some new books, some of them in Chinese, and some in foreign languages.'

I reflected on the years L and I had known each other, ever since the 70s: we'd once worked together, for the same newspaper during the day and on our own magazine after work. We used to write and translate poetry together. We'd shared so many common interests and beliefs. But real life had turned things sour, had made all our aspirations seem more and more of an illusion. We used to get together and discuss poetry and literature, we'd chat about every subject under the sun, and drink until we were well and truly away and there were no borders left in the entire world. But later, in that sober moment in the hospital, as we sat facing one another, each of us at a turning-point in our lives, weighed down by a host of difficult circumstances, with no clear path in sight, I couldn't help but feel for his plight as if it were my own.

L was eventually discharged from hospital and went back to work for a while, but shortly afterwards he couldn't cope with the pressure at work and had to be hospitalized once again. In the end he agreed to take a job in the publishing branch of a TV corporation, at a reduced salary. At least he was doing something he was familiar with. By then I'd been back in Hong Kong for a whole year, but not only was I finding it impossible to finish my dissertation, I was having all kinds of other problems of my own. So in the end I decided to go back to the USA for a year just to finish the dissertation. By the time I was about to leave, I was glad to observe that L's life was taking a turn for the better.

When I returned a year later, his job was already more or less back on track. He was working for a commercial publishing house, but still aimed to do something serious after office hours. He was busy reading thick biographies of famous foreign publishers, books his sister had sent him. He liked to talk about these publishers and how they'd gone out of their way to solicit new manuscripts and discover new talent. He spoke with great admiration of their vision and courage. We exchanged biographies of famous poets, and shared whatever reviews of foreign books had caught our attention. We spent many happy hours together in the bars, planning our future. I introduced him to some contemporary fiction and prose from mainland China, told him about new experiments that were taking place in the literary columns of the Hong Kong press, and about the New Fiction from Japan. It seemed unrealistic to hope to be detached from the commercial culture that surrounded us, so I thought we might as well try introducing something that could appeal to both elite and popular readers alike.

He seemed to be doing quite well, but when I left Hong Kong for New York in 1991, I vaguely sensed he was in trouble again. He told me his wife wanted to leave Hong Kong because of the threat posed by the 1997 hand-over, but if they did decide to emigrate to the US, he was concerned that he would have difficulty earning a living. I sensed that the cause of their estrangement and their quarrels was more complex than that. His wife also complained to me that he spent too much time in the bars, that he was drinking too much... Their differences seemed to stem from something deeper.

Now as I take up my pen again, I don't know what to say. When I saw his family I lied to them. I said that all was well with him, even though his sister had already guessed something from his literary columns in the newspapers, or had heard from friends that he and his wife had separated. L still had this foolish idea that his mother would not take the news well, so he'd never written or called the family. He'd promised to visit her in New York but then never came. He didn't realize that what he was doing only made his mother feel worse. I wanted to write and tell him this, but I didn't know if I was really capable of giving him anything useful in the way of advice. I had all along told him not to write about his private affairs in the press, but at the same time I had taken his articles myself to the publishing office of 'Breakthrough' magazine. I advised him not to drink too much, but then I ended up sitting and drinking with him. Many times I found myself criticizing him to his face, but deep down part of me couldn't help identifying with his feelings, even though I realized his emotionalism and his exaggerated romanticism were out of tune with the real world.

You told me you sent your daughter flowers, and she agreed to have dinner with you but never came. I feel sorry for you, but at the same time you should try and understand how hard it is for her to make choices the way things are. Quite apart from her family problems, the whole world in which she and her generation have grown up has inevitably shaped their perception of things. Think about it: in this society of ours, what can we point to that helps our children to grow up with good ideas, to make good judgements?

That's what concerns me: the whole mental climate in which we live.

Try looking at things in a different way: as an editor, if you do your job well, you can make a positive contribution to society...

What disturbs me is the way all these negative forces are damaging our quality of life, and destroying the basic goodness of people.

I don't know what else to say.

The other passengers have all boarded the bus, except for our small group and a woman from South America. We're waiting to be questioned by a Customs officer. My situation is simple enough. I went to New York to do some research six months ago, and now I am going back there, after spending a pleasant weekend with my family in Toronto. My friends G and F and their daughter — so I learned from a conversation of theirs that I overheard — are taking the bus to submit their immigration applications. They have a lawyer waiting to help them in Buffalo. The South American woman seems to be encountering more serious difficulties. They've been asking her where she spent her vacation and are searching her bags. Their attitude seems rather hostile and suspicious. She's still standing there with them as we all climb back onto the bus. Finally, about ten minutes later, she climbs on board the bus with her heavy bag, shaking her head dejectedly.

G sits down in the front of the bus next to his daughter, who puts on her headphones to avoid answering his questions. I had no idea he was applying to immigrate. I ran into him in Toronto, and he asked me about buses to Buffalo, which is how we ended up travelling together. It wasn't until our bus had almost reached the border that he finally told me the purpose of his trip. It was silly of him to want to keep it a secret. As if I would think poorly of him for wanting to immigrate! Among my circle of friends immigration is no longer even news. We are all concerned at the way things are evolving. I just wanted to ask him why he'd picked such an out-of-the-way place as Buffalo to submit his papers? But the bus had reached the actual border, and the driver asked everyone to take their luggage off for inspection. Border inspection here used to be very relaxed, so I've heard, but over the years they've tightened up. Too many people have been trying to take advantage of it. Our little group from Hong Kong becomes very nervous all of a sudden, even though there's no reason for us to be this way. Our reaction must have something to do with the acute hypersensitivity that most Hong Kong people have grown up with towards passports and visas and borders.

Once we used to march on the streets together, G and I, demanding that Chinese be made an official language in Hong Kong, protesting against injustice, proclaiming our beliefs. But that seems so far away now. These were journeys we shared, but we seem to have become reluctant to talk about them. Over the years, G has become a prominent figure, sought after by the media, involved in a lot of important decisions. I've had my reservations about his sensational style, I may even have written one or two articles in the press openly criticizing his style of media-manipulation. Even though I never mentioned him by name, the criticism was implicit. For some reason, anyway, we became estranged from each other afterwards. When we met again this time, at first I forgot about these incidents, and we were soon laughing and joking in the old way. But after a while, neither of us seemed to know how to keep the conversation going.

Now G leans back in his seat. He seems to be relaxed, or even asleep. It looks gloomy outside. In a short while the bus arrives in Buffalo.

For some reason Buffalo looks desolate. We walk down this street, from one end to the other, and finally find our hotel. Once they've settled in, their daughter wants to go out and buy a leather coat, but F suggests we should try to find the Immigration and Naturalization Bureau first. It's not far, just a few stops on the bus. On the way back we walk into a shopping mall. We all seem enormously tired. It's bitterly cold and the sky is grey. Some of the shops are closed already, and the daughter doesn't feel like talking because she hasn't found the leather coat she wanted. I originally thought we might have a good meal together. I'm leaving for New York the next morning, and they've decided to head back to Toronto once their paperwork is done. If our old habits of many years had been anything to go by, we'd have ended up spending a wild night drinking. But a lot of the seafood restaurants listed in the guide books are no longer there, and the Italian restaurants are closed too. Everyone seems very down and preoccupied, and in the end we decide to have a simple meal in the hotel restaurant. Night falls quickly. For some unknown reason we are all exhausted and don't much feel like talking. Since they have things to do the next morning, we say good night right after dinner. I manage to find an opportunity to ask G why he picked Buffalo to submit his application, and he replies that it was their immigration lawyer who told them to do it. Apparently it's faster to process applications from third countries than from HK. The fastest place of all is Italy. Submit an application from Italy, and you can get an interview with an immigration officer at once. That's the point. G says they don't *want* their application to go through so fast. Even now, as things stand, he says, it's going to be too fast. 'We want to immigrate quickly, but not *too* quickly.' Isn't this Hong Kong mentality of ours laughable! This last comment of his makes us all laugh, and for a while it's almost like the old days. Then we all go back to our rooms.

I stay a while in my room, feeling low and at a loose end. I don't want to go to sleep quite yet, so I start writing some letters. In the end I decide to go downstairs to the bar and have a drink, take my paper with me and carry on writing there. All sorts of letters. Unfinished letters.

L — when I got to New York, I went to visit your relations…

I carry manuscripts of my stories about with me wherever I go, and letters to reply to and all kinds of other scraps of writing. I lug them from one place to another, across borders. I never finish them. I'm a hopeless case.

A lot of people applying to immigrate really do move to other countries to lodge their papers. As for me, I just keep trundling unfinished letters around the world, bags full of waste paper, trundling them across borders, into and out of one country after another. And I always seem to be writing about the last place I've been to, or replying to letters delivered to some previous address. I'm always one step behind reality.

This is my last night in New York. It's midnight already, and I've just got back from a friend's home. I've had quite a few glasses of red wine and am feeling a bit light-headed. But I decide to do a little bit of packing and tidying up, to somehow mark the end of my six-month stay in the city.

I start by going over some books and papers. That's what I always seem to be doing: going over books and papers. I still haven't opened some of the boxes of books and other stuff that I shipped back to Hong Kong ten years ago. Ever since my return I've been busy with work, and even though I didn't actually travel abroad for many years, I never had the feeling of having settled down anywhere. Work wears you out, there's always so much 'urgent business' to be attended to. I've never had the time to reflect on the past or plan for the future. Both in my life and in my work, I seem to have been living in a community with which I feel no harmony. I have never received much support or recognition for what I have done. I started off with so many hopes and beliefs, but it seems in the end much of my effort has been wasted. I stand on the margins, forced by circumstances to fight against prejudice and misunderstanding as they present themselves. This work wears me out, but I still live in the hope that these little things may be able to bring about some slight change. Sometimes I don't even know if I am right about this.

It was years before I left Hong Kong again. As I revisited the cities I once stayed in during my travels I found myself thinking of the novel I have never finished revising. It's been hard to finish, because things have changed, because cities have changed, because I myself have changed. Over the years, I have gradually come to see another side of things. Sometimes bright colours have faded. I can see lightness as well as heaviness, I know how easily persistence can become obstinacy. I have grown cynical about some things that I once really believed in. As firmly held beliefs collapse, I have had to rethink everything from scratch. W, D and Y are no longer in the capital city where I once used to meet them. They are back in Hong Kong, they have been there for varying lengths of time. We have all had to abandon our holiday mood, our carefree ways, for real life. After my return to Hong Kong all those years ago, I discovered that many things had changed. The city was no longer a mutually supportive place for creative writers. This time, now that I've left again, a lot of people ask me about Hong Kong. It's strange. I always seem to defend Hong Kong when I'm away from it, and I always criticize it when I'm there. Perhaps this ambivalence comes from my constantly shifting perspective, my ever-changing location. Now, I'm packing yet again, preparing to return once more to Hong Kong. I suppose I no longer have the convictions and expectations of ten years ago. I just want to sit down, finally unpack the books I have bought, read them and reflect on my half year abroad. I want to be able to go over what I've written, have time to talk to my friends. Does this mean I am yearning to go 'home'? Wait a minute. I know that's something I won't find when I return to Hong Kong. I'm sure I'll just be thrown into new work, I'll be caught up in endless meetings, and have to deal with all kinds of problems. Who knows when all my boxes will ever be opened. But despite everything I really want to go back. Which doesn't stop me from making a detour through Eastern Europe, as if somehow that might postpone the date of my return…

I've undertaken this particular journey at the urging of a friend. Even as I sort out my books and papers and fold my few clothes, I am contemplating a new journey. All journeys end. I know. No matter how much we may want to keep on travelling, going to new places, seeing new things, no matter how badly we want to stay on the road, we also want — even more badly — to stop, to settle down in some kindly community, among familiar people, to find ourselves a space in which to live and work.

So we return to the city where we were born, where we grew up, the place where we have lived. But in the end we do not necessarily find what we are looking for. We are so easily pushed aside by the forces at work around us, pushed out to the margins of these closed communities. We are so often represented or misrepresented by others. We constantly hear other people speak for us and in the course of long-winded reports and plans find ourselves transformed into some non-existent entity.

This is when you may remember journeys taken long ago in the past, things seen and recorded while you were away. This is when you may feel like going over old scraps, old notes, in the hope that the new 'present' will make them seem interesting.

In the olden days every journey held a fascination, a meaning. Seafarers would project their fantasies of the world onto the strange maps they took with them on their travels, transforming unknown spaces into realms of wild conjecture. In fact, if the traveller does not take the time to examine the journey's hypothesis, some journeys end where they begin. And if fantasy is not tempered by reality, other journeys are fraught with real danger. The searchers of the 70s all seemed to have a passionate sense of destiny, they went down the road shouting with burning conviction. But right now, as I pack, I am more concerned about my journey home. What can I take back with me? Can I overcome the hardships of the journey, like Odysseus, can I master my desires and demons and return to a space of my own, a place that has not been expropriated, taken away from me? Or should I just follow the flow of language, should I just drift and let my own legend write itself? Words rise, with their infinite associations, they soar, they move endlessly on and outwards, never stopping to look down. Of course, you don't want to stop too soon, you don't want to take easy detours or give up before the end. But sooner or later you will reach a destination, you will sit down, sort out your things, marshal your thoughts. You can't drift for ever, and never come down to earth, never descend to the mortal plane.

'It's hard to believe your son is so grown up!'

'There's unfinished work to be done back home!'

'Whatever happened to the places and people we know?'

So you set off home. You pass through one city after another, you visit one friend after another, in the attempt to get back to your city, to the place where you used to live. Demons and monsters live, not on faraway islands, but in the very place to which you try to return but cannot. You hold onto memories, but in the end, one by one, they turn out to be empty illusions.

I remember the night before you left, for some strange reason we had a conversation about glass. You came out of the elevator, stood in the hallway, and made this statement: 'Glass is liquid. It flows downwards, continuously and slowly, which is why, after this process of precipitation, a piece of glass is thicker at the bottom than at the top.' I don't know whether this is true, but you are a science student, so you should be better informed than I am. After we went into the room we stopped talking about glass. I still can't remember exactly how we started this conversation about glass. It still bothers me. My memories are getting more and more confused. Which night was it? After a while, the days tend to cohere and become opaque. But some things still remain clear. Like the day we went to see 'Les Miserables', or the day we and our friends went to see the Wim Wenders film 'Till the World Ends'. Or the afternoon we saw 'Madame Bovary', and followed it up the same evening with 'Return to the Forbidden Planet'. Some days are memorable because of a play that you liked or a movie that I liked, or because we were with friends, or because the temperature suddenly dropped and it started snowing. I can never remember dates, or which day or week it was. I always begin by remembering that we went to see a dance performance in a church... And then I can remember it was a Monday. I remember one New Year's Eve we left Uncle Mo's home and walked toward 42nd Street with Uncle Lee. Then we crossed Times Square on our way home, and a girl said 'Happy New Year!'. Later you said New York didn't seem to be in much of a Christmas mood, but that was probably because I didn't take you to see the biggest Christmas tree in New York, or the brightest lights, or the most colourful window displays. I vaguely thought about taking you, but then everyone suggested going to a movie. So we hurried to the theatre, and on the way we stopped by a skating rink and gazed at the lights and sounds — but only for a very moment, just long enough for you to finish your hotdog. I'm sure a model father would have done a better job, but I'm not a model father and wouldn't want to pretend to be one. A model father would never have taken his son to see the Spanish movie 'High Heels'. The day before we'd seen those two old movies by Billy Wilder and enjoyed them, and you said how much you liked comedies, so I checked out the programmes and this was the nearest thing I could find to a comedy. I'd seen other pieces by this director and they'd been very funny. How was I to know that this particular movie would turn out so differently? Later, every time you remembered this incident, you made fun of me. What can I say — I made a mess of things… I did have plans for our vacation, but then what with everything that was going on, all the changes that were happening every day, I had to keep adding and subtracting things here and there, I had to somehow find a compromise between your interests and mine, to keep constantly adjusting my original ideas to the real life situation. It was a fluid process… Anyway, we ended up going to a lot of movies together. You said you wanted to see all sorts of different types of movies, which was a relief. If you'd said you wanted to find out more about space or nuclear physics, I'd have been hard put to it, even if I'd gone to the library and done some reading. I'm not anti-science. Cross my heart. Didn't I take you to see the dinosaurs? I know I left you half way and ran to 46th Street to check out the Broadway tickets for that night, but I did go back later and finish the tour of the aquarium with you, didn't I? When I think back to that day (see, I *am* capable of self-reflection!) I admit that probably all I said about the aquarium was that Woody Allen had used it to good effect as a location in 'Manhattan'. I suppose I should have given you a long lecture about the species of shark we were looking at, and how its teeth differed structurally from other species. (You see, I'm quite capable of self-reflection. I always was…) I think my generation (or is it just me?) learned to perceive the world as a series of shots from a movie. It wasn't until we were in our thirties and forties that we realized how many things there were in the real world that we simply didn't know how to deal with. On the one hand, we seemed to be so knowledgeable about human nature and the affairs of men; on the other, we were like primary school kids, we had to learn from scratch how to live. Take Uncle Mo, for instance. He gave up his business and emigrated to the US with his family. Then he had to start all over again. He had to go back to school and find a job. One of the family fell ill and died. I greatly admired his courage in surmounting all these obstacles. Ever since you were little I've never tried to stuff you full of extra information about literature and culture, I always hoped you'd learn to cope with everyday life like an ordinary person, not like us. I may have gone a bit too far in this other direction. But I could never be a father figure like the one depicted in the translator Fu Lei's letters to his son. I've never thought I should set up a strict model for you to base yourself on — no matter how good that model might be. I have always wanted you to have the space to develop on your own, even if that means making mistakes and following all sorts of detours, perhaps taking a longer time to reach your destination. Even the best map in the world can never guarantee that we will not end up in a cul-de-sac. In real life the roads are not like the ones we talk about or the ones we imagine. Other children's fathers show their affection by driving their sons to the tennis club or to other activities. We were different. We were a couple of clowns, always taking the subway to off-off-Broadway shows. In the end, everyone has a different path to follow. That's why every time we come out of the subway, I always ask you to look around (you see things so much more clearly at your age than we do; we are peering through our lenses all the time…) and tell me which way is 56th Street and which is 58th Street. I have to confess that without identifiable landmarks I'm quite useless. I can walk several blocks before discovering that I've been walking in the wrong direction, that the place I was absolutely sure was in front of me is actually behind me, and I have to retrace my steps. You laughed at me when I lost my way on one occasion. (But I assure you, among my friends I am far from being the most confused …) I can only say that the lesson to be learned from getting lost is this: reality does not always fit with our mental blue-print. Today's lesson is this: I could very easily get lost again.

As I am writing this, the shadow cast by my lampshade is swinging across my words, back and forth, like reflections on water, illuminated ripples, as if the words themselves have become evanescent and changeable. Uncle

Lee is sitting next to me. We are passing the early hours together in this Polish border town writing letters, waiting for the dawn. Once again our romantic journey has been thwarted by reality. Anyway, for whatever reason, we have failed to get our visas for Czechoslovakia. Partly laziness, partly procrastination, partly impatience with bureaucracy. We thought maybe we wouldn't need a visa, or maybe we could get one in Hungary. But we were thrown off the train when it passed through a small town on the Czech border with Poland. So tomorrow we have to go back to Warsaw for our visas, and make the same journey all over again, there and back. No matter what we said, nothing worked. We even agreed not to get off the train anywhere in Czechoslovakia... And Uncle Lee has a Hong Kong British National (Overseas) Passport. It was no use at all. There's nothing romantic about being from Hong Kong, I thought to myself, as I dragged my heavy suitcase through the snow and mud of the streets of this border town.

Now we are sitting here, exhausted but incapable of sleeping, one at each end of a long table, sipping hot tea and writing letters. Sometimes confused grown-ups like us manage to egg each other on into doing some work. So I write and write. I sometimes want to tell you everything, all the thoughts I've had as I wander across all kinds of borders. Would these thoughts be of any use to you when I'm not beside you, when you continue to travel? I know that there's nothing everlasting about words. In fact, I prefer the shifting shadows cast by the lamplight. Yesterday when I couldn't sleep I stared at the ceiling, at the waves of light thrown by the passing cars, constantly opening and closing like a fan. I may not remember every day that has gone by, but I do remember the occasional effect of light and shade.

It is a good thing we were able to go to the movies when you were in New York this summer. After I'd left you at the airport, the room felt suddenly very empty, and it took me a while to adjust to my new condition. I remember that night we went to a Spanish restaurant to have paella. Strangely though I've forgotten the name of the play we saw before dinner. But I remember taking a walk with you afterwards in the cold, and then having dinner with you and some of our conversation. Yes, even as I write, memories come flooding back. It was Shakespeare's 'As you Like It' at the Pearl Theatre. Afterwards, I asked you why you'd wanted to watch a Shakespeare play, and whether you'd found it difficult to follow. You seemed very bright and cheerful that day, you seemed to want to talk a lot. Maybe it was something to do with the paella? Maybe. Maybe not. To really say anything, one has to start somewhere, one has to let the words come, let it all out. Our conversations have been the way I've come to know you better. I haven't really thought about it like this before. You once told me about a classmate of yours in Hong Kong who became obsessed with a popular writer's romantic novels, stories of young people in love. As a result, in his own life and loves he always sought for passion, he wanted to behave according to these extreme models of loyalty and true love, and found the actual conditions of real life unacceptable. Is it this sort of example that has caused you to think more deeply, to be more curious about things? I myself have been obsessed with the world of the lens, and have thereby lost touch with reality. I know what it feels like to walk into that hard wall, like the scientist in 'Return to the Forbidden Planet', or Prospero and his obsession with books in 'The Tempest'. That's why I've never insisted on your reading or watching movies. I would have been perfectly happy for you to be more interested in science or computer studies. Listening to pop music or watching screwball comedy movies will make you a more balanced, normal person. There's really no need to be different, to be a loner. But now I know you've reached a stage when those easy options are no longer enough. You want to know more about the world, you want to go beyond existing boundaries, to expand your horizons, and find something else to balance those superficial impulses. We talked about the tragedy of Emma in 'Madame Bovary', about the novelist in 'Until the End of the World', who tells his story in a complex series of overlapping images, a nightmarish mirage of narcissism. We talked and talked. You said a lot, and so did I. I drank wine, you drank Coke. I didn't get drunk, just a bit tipsy. We were like family members meeting for a bite to eat after a very long journey. Our words drifted into the distance, then veered round and returned to make contact again. We were truly a family sitting down to have dinner together. I'm glad you came here this time. We should spend another vacation together like this one of these days (it doesn't matter where), watch some plays, have dinner together again.

Islands and Continents

■ *Translated by Caroline Mason*

1.

There was really no way I could do any more reading, so I thought I'd go down to the beach again. Normally I never go downstairs without checking the mailbox. But this time, to avoid my landlady and her unstoppable banter, I decided to go out by the door on the other side. I walked on a little way, but it was no good, I couldn't put it out of my mind. I turned back and went to open the mailbox. It was only then that I really gave up all hope. My behaviour was a bit neurotic. It certainly must have looked pretty odd to anyone watching. To be honest, just at that moment I don't think I was capable of coping with anyone in real life.

I'd reached the sea, when a woman dressed in black came up to me and asked if I had a car. I was surprised by the question. She told me she was in a hurry to get somewhere, and I said no, I didn't have a car, but she just kept walking beside me. She looked so delicate, so thin and pale. She walked beside me for a while in silence, and then went on her way. Something about her fragile appearance had me worried, but there was not much I could do about it. I walked straight on to the entrance of the Museum of Contemporary

Art and stood there, looking at Zuniga's bronzes. His women either squat or sit, or else they stand there proudly, cradling a child in their arms, weather-beaten earth mothers, their bronze mottled and fading, their feet planted firmly in the soil. They keep their babies warm with the heat of their bodies, and carry their heavy woven baskets high on their shoulders. Never weak or helpless, never mutable or fragile. Their broad, green shoulders, corroded, laden with fallen pine needles, utterly immobile. I stood there, leaning against the railings, just gazing at them. Many a time I've wanted to try and tell you what it is I see in these women of Zuniga's, their special quality, but I've never been able to find the words.

After that, I went down to the beach, descending the stone steps just in time to see the sun slip into the ocean. Sunsets here are a beautiful sight, on this huge American continent where I now reside, with its unbroken coastline stretching endlessly into the distance. But it is a beauty I am rarely in the mood to appreciate. In front of me lay the vast, boundless ocean, and further out, lost in a haze of mist and cloud, the faint outlines of islands came into view. Seabirds wheeled before my eyes as I stood there in the breeze, my mind ebbing and flowing with thoughts of people and events on another dim, distant shore. I spoke to the ocean's vast expanse but heard nothing in reply. Again and again, all I heard was the sound of the waves curling their tongues in on themselves in self-absorption, and the muffled mutterings of the shingle. The sea was too deeply engrossed in the expression of its own thoughts to have ears for the babbling of some other creature's imagination. The noise of the tide grew louder and louder, drowning my voice, rendering my incessant chattering utterly redundant.

The young man put down his pen and gazed blankly out of the window. The ship was sailing slowly out across the vast body of water. The sun was creating little flashes of white light on the surface of the sea. Warm sunshine, gentle waves. A young woman was sitting out on deck near the rails, her head tilted slightly to one side. A gust of wind sent her hair blowing all over the place, and she quickly raised her hands high above her head to tie it back, her sleeves slipping down to reveal the white skin of her slender arms.

She rose to her feet and went towards the front of the ship, standing there with her hands on her hips, gently swinging her right leg backwards and forwards. Her supple limbs seemed to move with a rhythm of their own, and for a time she was utterly absorbed in this almost gymnastic movement. But then she turned and smiled at him, beckoning to him to come over to her. She pointed ahead, and together they gazed intently at the islands as they came into view.

Then it came back to me, the nightmare which had woken me with such a start that morning. I seemed to be a child again, and was being given a severe telling-off. I had no idea why such a trivial episode should have come and sought me out again after all this time. In fact I'd already forgotten the details. I just remembered that something had scared me and then I woke up. I don't know if I screamed or not. All of a sudden, all these people on the beach seemed to turn and look at me. Or perhaps they didn't. I don't remember how I walked back, I just remember having a splitting headache, as if there was a voice talking inside my head and I couldn't make out what it was saying. I'd already given up hope, so it came as a total surprise to see the blue shape in the mailbox. I opened the box immediately, but it wasn't the letter I'd been hoping for, it wasn't from her, it was from my mother. I walked upstairs and found a message on my door from a Chinese student in my department, inviting me to spend the holiday with him. What holiday? I even seemed out of touch with the passing of time. Mother had written to say that Uncle wanted her to lend him money. It wasn't the first time she'd written about it. She said she was going to try and take out a loan on his behalf, or else he'd have nowhere to live. I've always suspected him of cheating her, but it's no good, I'm so far away on the other side of the world, there's an ocean between us, I can't make her understand what's going on. In the long run I'm afraid she'll get into trouble herself and run up debts she'll never be able to pay back. I do worry about her, so far away; so I took out a sheet of paper to write to her, but after I'd written a few lines I tore it up. Outside the window it had grown dark. I hadn't noticed the light fade. For a moment I couldn't think where I was.

They were standing on the quay below a large temple, close to the railings. They were a boat's length apart, facing in different directions. The woman was watching the fishing boats, motionless on the sea to her left, while the man was looking back up the hill, watching a line of seven or eight people as they climbed up to look at the old rock carvings. After a while he moved closer to the woman, drew level with her, then walked on a few steps. He stood there below the temple and looked up at the temple-flags, which for some reason never stopped flapping. Someone wanted to take a photo, so he stepped back out of the way and stood against the railing, kicking idly at a piece of sodden litter which had lodged itself beneath the metal rail.

The man glanced silently in the woman's direction. He turned back, to look up at the people climbing the hill, watching them as they wound their way upwards and disappeared over the top. He watched for a while, then moved away from the railings and started to walk up the stone steps himself, as if he too intended to climb the hill. Halfway up, level with the large temple, he stopped and turned back once more. The woman was still standing by the railings, with her back to him. She had not moved. He sat down on the stone steps.

In a little while, he walked back, past the tourists brandishing their bamboo walking sticks and taking photos. He stood there against the railings again, at some distance from the woman. They gazed in different directions. He kicked at something beneath the railings, this time a pineapple someone had dropped on the ground. She turned round. Her eyes were red, as if she'd been crying.

He gazed blankly out of the window into the brooding darkness, into a space that seemed filled both with an enormous freedom and with a restless sense of anxiety and foreboding. He seemed to be dwelling in a total vacuum, to have lost touch with everyone and everything. He walked over to the fridge, meaning to take out some meat and defrost it, but in the end all he did was pour himself a glass of wine. If he was hungry he should cook something, and if he was sleepy he should go to bed. He knew that. But at that moment he was neither hungry nor sleepy. He just kept gazing aimlessly out of the window into the vast, infinite darkness, as if somehow in his mind he could conjure a rich spectrum of colour from the flooding, unbroken gloom of night.

The ship passed slowly through a gap between two hills, and everyone leaned over the sides to look at them. A man with a megaphone was giving a running commentary, telling all sorts of stories about features of the landscape. He explained that there were temples on both sides to Tin Hau Goddess of the Sea, one large and one small, and as the ship moved on they both came into view. The temple on one side was packed with worshippers — mostly women with children in tow, the mothers totally absorbed in consulting fortune-tellers or saying their prayers, the children playing happily and making a lot of noise. A pall of incense smoke curled gracefully into the sky above the general commotion. The temple on the other side appeared deserted — the doors were all closed and it was impossible to detect a single soul within the temple precinct. The man with the megaphone explained that in ancient times the two temples had been joined together. He quoted an old saying: 'When the bell is struck in the southern hall, it rings in the northern hall; when paper money is lit in the northern hall, smoke rises from the southern hall.' The ship sailed slowly on between the two temples, which were now separated by water.

I know what I should be doing now is concentrating on writing my thesis. But I just don't seem able to put my mind to it. I'm thinking of going to that conference in Shenzhen this summer. When I first came to the US in 1979, you and I used to talk about all the changes that were happening in China, Then you graduated and went home ahead of me. Since then you're the one who's been keeping me up to date. I've been vaguely following the direction things are taking, and now I'd like to go back and see for myself. Of course, I know what you're bound to say: I'm really going back to see her, now that she's back in Hong Kong. You're right. Nothing escapes your eagle eyes. The university may not even pay for my travel expenses. And my scholarship for next year hasn't been confirmed yet. You probably think I'm being very unrealistic, don't you? The truth is I've been away too long. I really do need to go back.

2.

I showed my mother the book of landscape photos I'd bought.

'Is that what it used to look like?'

'No, it's changed such a lot since then, I don't even recognize the place,' she said, leafing through the photos. 'There was nothing like *that*!' She was pointing at one of the modern buildings, a bit like the Zhufeng Hotel.

'And nothing like this, either.' Mother was pointing at the lock gates.

'Was there a place called Palm Village?' I asked.

'No, just a few places where they grew palms.'

As she leafed through the photographs, every now and then Mother would read out the name of a place that was familiar to her. 'Ah, yes — Mt. Gudou!'

'Have you been there?' I asked.

'Oh, yes. That's where we went when we were evacuated during the Anti-Japanese War.'

'It says in the book that it used to be a bandit hide-out. Is that true?'

'Yes, it's true.'

Mother was looking closely at a picture of Huicheng.

'Our old home was there in the town. But the streets were wider than they are in this photo. We lived in a big house, much bigger than this one.' She told me how her father had built a house on the edge of the lake. 'He always hoped to go home one day and claim it back. But a few years ago someone came out from the Mainland and told him that the house had been demolished. Some sort of government offices had been built on the site. So everything would have been different anyway.

'Every year he used to say we'd go back the next year.'

I remember how when I was little, and we lived on the south of the Island, at Wong Chuk Hang, Aberdeen, every October the newspapers that my grandfather subscribed to, the *Hong Kong Times* and *Overseas Chinese Daily*, used to give away free Nationalist flags. The papers always carried a front-page message from Chiang Kai-shek in big red characters, announcing a Taiwan counter-offensive against the Mainland. Grandfather always looked so proud. He kept repeating, 'Next year! It'll definitely be next year!' Grandfather was the great authority in the family. Every day, my uncles had to wait until he'd finished with the papers before they could read them, so of course I never got a look at all. After all, I was just a daughter's son, an outsider, taking shelter under his roof. I didn't think much of all that fancy political claptrap anyway. I just wanted to read the supplements, the love stories, the gossip columns, cartoons and jokes. Grandfather maintained some of his old Mainland habits: he valued his sons more than his daughters, he 'treasured the old and despised the new'. He ruled the family from on high, with a degree of pomp and ritual. He was an accomplished chess player and a fine calligrapher in the standard style. He used to write couplets and scrolls for people at New Year, and go out with his geomancer's compass to find the best Fengshui spots for an ancestral grave. He could recite the *Thousand Character Classic* and the *Three Character Classic* by heart, and declaimed Han prose-poems and Six Dynasties parallel prose in ringing tones. But none of it moved me at all.

I never had any playmates when I was little, I just liked to hide away on my own in the tin hut in the village which we used as a store-room. It had a whole roomful of books which my parents had brought with them from the Mainland, their little library of modern Chinese literature. Apparently my father had also brought with him some good old-fashioned political ideals. But faced with the realities of life in Hong Kong he had become very depressed and disillusioned. In the commercially-minded society of this small border island he had been unable to find a job that would allow him to fulfil his aspirations, and in the end his frustration reached such a pitch that he fell ill and died prematurely. At the time I was still too young to understand much at all. I would try working my way respectfully through his tomes of political essays and translations of literary criticism. But they were full of incomprehensible expressions, and I never managed to get very far. I actually preferred my mother's books, things like Zhu Shenghao's translations of

Shakespeare and Zhu Xiang's anthology of foreign poetry, *The Guava Collection*. They may have been translations, but for me the characters in those books were alive. They kept me company as I idled away whole afternoons, with the sun sinking lazily in the sky. They whispered in my ear in the moments before I fell asleep.

Mother was the traditional devoted daughter and virtuous wife, with all the qualities of Bai Yan, 'White Swallow', the Hong Kong film star of the fifties and sixties. She always did her best in every situation, even if she herself was treated unfairly. She didn't seem to have the words to tell her own story, but found sustenance in radio soaps, Cantonese dramas and even romantic Hollywood movies. She was a very practical person, someone who tried hard to make a living within the limits imposed by her actual situation, taking all sorts of work to make ends meet. I remember she made plastic flowers, stuck together match boxes, and for a while threaded beads for ornamental belts. These were all jobs farmed out by small wholesalers, piece-work for housewives who slaved away at home for a pittance. Mother was not at all stuck-up about having had a good education. She didn't mind doing this sort of thing. As she threaded great piles of beaded belts, she used to compete with her sisters, reciting poems from the Tang and Song dynasties. The lively, down-to-earth setting, with manual work going on all around, gave the ancient words an added vitality.

Later, Mother left the village to look for a job in the city. The old system was still in force, and men and women were still paid different wages for doing the same work. In the end she managed to find a job teaching in a primary school run by a welfare association in Mongkok. It was no mean achievement. My grandparents thoroughly disapproved, and hardly ever spoke about their eldest daughter, although it was she, more than any other member of the family, who had proved capable of adapting to all the gradual changes that were taking place in the urban society of our small border island. I stayed in the village while Mother went to work in the city on her own. From the clothes and possessions of the others around me, from the quality of their meals, and from the decisions made whenever there were quarrels, I became sensitive to my plight, to what it was to be a dependent. Mother came back every weekend, bringing movie magazines and the latest toys from the city. But then after that would come another week for me of solitary reading, and of imagining, from the pages I read, the better, or worse, worlds that might exist beyond our village.

When I walked by myself along the small road in front of our house, on my way to catch beetles in the fields of vegetables, sometimes I'd look up at the top of Nam Long Mountain and see kites wheeling high in the sky. I knew nothing about the outside world. People told me that kites snatched baby chicks, but I'd never seen it for myself. They also told me that it was against the law to eat kites, because the word for kite in Chinese — *ying* — had the same sound as the word for Britain, and Hong Kong was under British rule. I had a rather hazy impression of Britain, knowing only that it was somewhere on another continent far far away. Apart from that there was the Coronation, and the parades and carnival in Aberdeen. I don't remember the details, I only remember that everyone got given a grey aluminium Coronation tooth-mug. I used mine, afterwards, to keep the worms I dug up in the fields.

I also remember once eating kite meat. It was a kite that had got lost, and for some reason had flown into the tin hut, the one where we kept the books. There it flailed around, panic-stricken, in the labyrinth of old Chinese tomes. None of us children were allowed in, but the few able-bodied menfolk that were still left in the village went in, shut the door and engaged the bird in combat. Much later, when we had forgotten all about it, we were told that they had succeeded in catching it. At the dinner table that night, each branch of the family was presented with a few lumps of some horrible, indeterminate substance. It was tough as old boots, rubbery in texture and absolutely tasteless, so no one would eat it.

So, my only childhood impressions of Britain, and its far-away continent, were of a shiny grey aluminium tooth-mug and some weird tasteless old meat.

Only a couple of weeks after I came back from the United States, I was showing a visitor round Hong Kong and we went to the area on the southern part of the island where I had lived as a child. The village no longer existed, but Nam Long Mountain was still there. Working my way back from the angle at which I could remember seeing the mountain in my childhood, I was able to calculate that where our old home had once been was now the main entrance to Ocean Park. I looked up again at Nam Long Mountain, but there were no longer kites wheeling in the sky, only cable cars shuttling back and forth high above. The village where I had lived as a child had disappeared. The old manual livelihoods had given way to the newly developed real estate and tourist business, and wherever I looked I saw block after block of high-rise buildings constructed with foreign capital.

It wasn't a happy experience for me as a child, living in the grim shadow of my maternal grandfather. I started to rebel at an early age, and after I moved out to live with Mother I was never keen to go back and visit grandfather and the rest of the family. Every time Mother went there, I tried to find an excuse not to go with her. I didn't want to see them, and when I did see them I didn't want to talk to them. When I got to university and started to write, I chose to go in a direction which was culturally and politically the opposite of theirs.

My very first trip back to the Mainland was in 1974, at the tail-end of the Cultural Revolution. In my small hotel we had to start queuing for dinner at five in the afternoon. Tired strips of cloth inscribed with anti-Lin Biao and anti-Confucius slogans hung around us in the gloomy hall, as we bent our heads and ate our coarse rice in silence. I took care not to leave anything on my plate. The first time I crossed the border at Lo Wu, gun-toting PLA soldiers sternly inspected our suspect passports and swore contemptuously when they saw that in the box marked 'Purpose of Visit' we had written the word 'Tourism'. This stern gaze of theirs seemed to follow me wherever I went. Late that evening I found a place to stay in a small hotel on a dimly lit street. I didn't manage to sleep at all that night, and lay there on a makeshift bed in the corridor listening to the various small noises around me. On a crowded bus I had my pocket picked. It was all a totally different world from the Chinese civilization I had read about. You couldn't really call what I was doing 'tourism': each time I wanted to go from one place to another I had to file an application, clutching my Home Return Permit and other documents, and I was never able to travel very far. That stern gaze followed me everywhere. It made me want to shrink into nothing. I hoped that if I attempted to merge myself with all the blue-grey and make myself as inconspicuous as possible, nobody would notice my existence.

My childhood spent in my grandfather's extended family had taught me how to conceal myself in this way. But despite my efforts the stern gaze never let up. When I left the country they rummaged mercilessly through my luggage and removed photos I'd taken — for inspection. Apparently I had shown insufficient respect for their magnificent buildings, and for the hoardings pasted with slogans.

When the train crossed the border into the New Territories, I felt as if a great burden had finally been lifted from me. Arriving at the station in Tsimshatsui, I was so happy to be home, and went straight to the bookshop in Ocean Terminal to see what new books and magazines had come in. It was just an ordinary foreign-language bookshop frequented mostly by tourists, but I always managed to find my favourite underground magazines and anthologies of poetry, things that had somehow slipped through the net and got in from the outside world. I chose what I wanted and then bore my treasures off to the Brazilian coffee shop on the first floor, where I ordered a cup of strong coffee. On my way there I looked through the round windows in the doors and glimpsed the exotic inscriptions on the sides of the great ocean-going liners moored at the quayside beyond — mysterious words from distant worlds.

Mother absolutely insisted that I should go and see him before I left to study in the United States, so, very unwillingly, I went. He was lying in a deck chair, his hair much whiter than it had been, his face markedly thinner. Mother said he had been sitting in the chair like this every day, staring into space, ever since he first fell ill six months or so earlier. Sometimes, to save electricity, he went a whole day without turning on the light, just sitting there in the dark, with who knows what thoughts running through his head. There was a crowd of children making a racket outside the house that day, so although his mouth opened, I couldn't hear what he was saying. I noticed that he had lost several teeth. They used to be so strong. He always loved eating sugar-cane and chewing pork bones.

'In the old days the big house was very grand. There were fruit-trees and flowers everywhere in the garden. Now there's nothing left.' Mother went on, 'He was in the palm-leaf fan business, and used to ship the goods up to Jiangxi province for sale. There were some valuable ceramic pieces in the sitting-room which he brought back from Jiangxi, with his name fired onto them. These days that's nothing special — but back then, it was very rare.'

'How ill is he, really?'

She shook her head.

'He just sits there at home every day, except for when he goes to see the doctor.'

I think of him sitting there silently in his deck chair, in the corner of the room, his eyes gazing in front of him, as if into empty space. It was impossible to tell what he was seeing. He seemed to be waiting for something, without knowing what it was. If you went closer, you could see that his eyes were actually closed. He would frequently sit there like that for a whole day.

3.

We finally met again at a translators' conference in Shenzhen. We noticed each other on the ferry. He raised his hand rather shyly. That was all he could manage by way of a greeting. We'd been writing to each other all through the years since we'd last been together, and had kept up with each other's lives, but on this occasion the boat tickets had been purchased as a group booking and our seats were some distance apart. So at that instant, in front of all the others, we just behaved like casual acquaintances and weren't really able to express our feelings at seeing each other again. I observed him from a distance. He was sitting between two passengers, both strangers, staring out through the windows, past the cabin and its hubbub, at the vast expanse of sea and sky.

When we had disembarked and were going through customs, I spotted him in the crowd and went to stand at the back of his queue, separated from him by two other people. He seemed rather nervous and kept taking his travel documents out of his pocket and putting them back again. He stood there in a daze, paying a lot of attention to the stamping process going on at the counter ahead of him, and forgetting to move forward with the queue. He seemed to hesitate, as if he really wanted to stay where he was and not have to walk through and be immersed, all at once, in a new world he had never set foot in before. We were next to each other as we climbed onto the minibus that came to meet us, and again on arrival at the hotel, when we went to the reception desk to register for the conference, but we didn't manage to have a proper talk. He still seemed very pre-occupied, and what little conversation we did have was very disjointed.

He sat beside me on the bus and I noticed that whenever we passed a new building, or a patch of empty waste ground on a hillside, or a university campus under construction, he would stare at it intently. He scrutinized the factory districts beside the road, even a sign pointing to a resort hotel.... I had already seen such things, and now I just followed his gaze, trying to work out what was going through his mind. He seemed desperate to devour everything he saw; but then again, it might have been nothing more than a normal form of absorbed enthusiasm, or maybe the scenery was simply whizzing past him like the pages of a book, and nothing special was actually going in at all.

Because we arrived at the same time, we were put in the same room. At dinner that evening, when everyone else was being very jolly and constantly urging him to drink, he cut a sorry figure. He accepted other people's cards, but he was no good at introducing himself and just sat quietly to one side. He started asking a question about translators of romantic literature, but the conference participants seemed to know little about the subject. They were more interested in research in linguistics and applied translation, and kept asking him about the latest developments overseas. A lecturer researching Hong Kong and Taiwanese literature was holding forth about the novels of some female writer he thought was first-rate when he blurted out very rudely that he failed to see the significance of that sort of popular literature. When we went back to our room after the meal, he moved an arm-chair across to the window and sat looking blankly out into the dark street below. Later on, when the people from the room next to ours came and knocked at the door to say there was no water in their bathroom, and then when all the lights suddenly went out at midnight (someone said there'd been a power shortage), he showed not the slightest interest or concern and simply carried on sitting there in silence.

Lying on my bed in the darkness I asked him when he'd returned to Hong Kong, but all he would tell me was that he'd just got back and had recently been to see a doctor. I'd seen him taking some pills which he told me were tranquillizers. I remembered all his warm-hearted letters to me of the past, in which he'd written about how much he missed his friends, and asked me what I thought about all the changes that were taking place in China. Sometimes he wrote heatedly for or against some issue. Now, for some reason, he seemed frozen and silent, totally withdrawn. He looked so tired and haggard, but when I told him to go to bed he just shook his head.

In the middle of the night I became aware of a light shining in my eyes: the electricity had come back on, and there he was writing a letter. He apologized and I thought he meant about the light having woken me up, so I told him not to worry about it. Suddenly he asked how much it would cost to send a letter to Hong Kong and when I told him, he asked if I had any stamps. Of course I hadn't. I suggested he should buy some from the girl at the desk in the morning. I watched him fold a pile of paper and put it into a long envelope, then I turned over and went back to sleep. As I dozed off, I heard the sound of paper being torn up. He must have been writing like this all night, because the next morning when I woke up he was still crouched over the desk.

The next day, he didn't attend the opening ceremony, but lay low in our hotel room all day. That night he kept the light on and wrote letters again. When I got up to go to the bathroom, he gave me an awkward smile, as if he knew very well that he had done something he shouldn't have, but couldn't help it. I came back, sat on the edge of the bed, and lit a cigarette. When he looked round and asked if I was having trouble sleeping, I couldn't restrain myself from asking him straight out how a certain person was, and whether the two of them had seen each other.

His reply was very confused, and I was only vaguely able to understand a few snatches of what he was saying. I learned that he'd waited all day in the lobby of her building, but the rest I couldn't make head or tail of: something about new towns, satellite towns, new mini-supermarkets, and conservative ordinary families on the Island. He seemed to be trying to argue that these new living spaces were somehow linked to emotional changes in people's lives. What it boiled down to was apparently the fact that he'd waited for her at her office, feeling a complete fool. She'd agreed to meet him and then stood him up, time and again. She told him to phone her, and then started loudly repeating his entreaties back at him down the phone, apparently turning his infatuation into a sort of status symbol with which to impress her business associates at her end of the line. As he became less insistent and weakened, she began denying that there had ever been any sort of understanding between them. Finally it reached the stage where she refused to answer his calls. As he spoke to me, going into all these harrowing details one by one, his composure deserted him. He was at a loss to understand why things had changed like this. He'd only been away a few years, and his feelings were as strong as before. He'd come back to our little island hoping to be able to clear up any misunderstandings and start afresh, but hadn't realized that everything had changed. In the context of the new reality that now confronted him, the reality of the 1980s, old-fashioned, over-intense, cloying emotions such as his were regarded with cynicism. He had eventually managed to find out the phone number of the new place she'd moved to, on one of the outlying islands, but when he dialed it a male voice answered the phone. On the boat he'd started hearing strange clicking noises in his head. He suddenly rushed out of our room, with tears pouring down his face. I followed him out, but he howled at me to leave him in peace, so I had to turn back. Around dawn, I eventually heard him open the door and come back in.

The next day his face was very pale, and during the lectures he was restless and fidgety. One of the speakers had got half-way through a lecture and was repeating a sentence which had just been given as an example of identical words having different meanings in different cultures, when suddenly my friend stood up and walked out. It would have been easy to conclude, from this kind of behaviour, that he was fed up with everything around him, disenchanted with what he was seeing and hearing. You would have had to observe him closely to have noticed that in fact his intense gaze was not directed at the world before his eyes — he was not watching the streets crammed with vendors and their stalls, nor was he looking at the shifty character who came up to us and wanted to exchange our Hong Kong dollars, nor at the display of bad temper on the part of one of the drivers. Likewise, he didn't seem to care less about the arrangements at the conference, or whether the speakers kept to time, or had prepared properly, or left things out or strayed from the point. It was something else altogether. He'd come back to the East his heart bursting with cherished memories. He had failed to find the person he'd been longing for night and day during his absence. He had lost the only means of realizing his dreams. He had nothing left to hold on to. He was stepping into a void. He walked slowly down a small brightly lit street full of hawkers with no local money in his pockets and without even knowing what the correct exchange rate was. There was no way he could exchange his emotions for actual currency, so when he bought simple everyday articles or snacks, he was either badly ripped off or had people screaming at him. He seemed to be quite incapable of any normal form of transaction with this world.

On another occasion, he sat silent and pre-occupied in the conference-hall, beside an elderly translator. In the old days, the two of us used to go hunting for old magazines together, read new translations and reviews full of critical insights, but this time he seemed to have none of the old excitement left, nothing to share any more. There had been an interval of more than thirty years, and the man I was encountering now seemed quite different from the man I had once known. The elderly translator was talking about the arrangements that had been made for us in Guangzhou, the meals and hotel and so on, when suddenly my friend got up and walked away again, without a word. Perhaps the older man misconstrued this, thinking that he had no time for practical details, and couldn't be bothered to haggle over prices. Or perhaps he just found this strange visitor from abroad incomprehensible, and put his odd behaviour down to the vagary of some mood of his. Confronted with this new and complex reality, my friend suddenly seemed to be carried back by the tumult of his emotions into his own private world. We were all eating our congee one breakfast time, and having a desultory conversation about machine translation, when suddenly he launched off on some train of thought, something to do with his relatives in the Mainland, whispering to me wistfully that he'd never expected members of his own family to be so mercenary and materialistic.

A couple of days later, we went our separate ways: I was continuing north by train with some of the others to another conference. He told me privately that he couldn't bear it any longer and was going back. Maybe he meant he couldn't bear the torture of his infatuation any longer. I found myself wondering if he would ever be able to adjust the fever of his idealized passion to the cold realities of the present. He took his medication at the breakfast table, washing his rainbow-coloured pills down with the bland white congee. We said goodbye at the railway station. As the train moved off, some of the academics sitting opposite me started a heated discussion about the difficulty of finding equivalent phrases with which to translate simple expressions of emotion into an unfamiliar culture. An academic from the north of China mentioned as an interesting example a novel which had in fact already been translated into Chinese on our little island back in the sixties, but I didn't pick him up on it, because at that very moment I looked back and

saw the lonely figure of my friend fade into the distance, swallowed up by
the piles of luggage, household goods, nylon carrier bags, the tide of humanity.

4.

*Once again I was walking along the road towards the Art Museum, and as I
walked I thought about the last letter I wrote you. Do you still remember?
I'd never be able to tell you how much comfort those statues of Zuniga's
always used to give me. That's what I said. But the incredible thing is, this
time, as soon as I got there, I discovered that they'd all gone, those great
bronzes that had seemed so timelessly rooted in the soil! Those solid figures,
those emblematic earth-mothers, which gave us such comfort, such a sense
of permanence — even they were capable of suddenly vanishing without a
trace! A board in front of the museum announced a new exhibition. I walked
inside to find fragmented signs, broken lines, random blobs of colour,
strangely beautiful compositions which bore no relation to the outside world.
It was all two-dimensional. We will never again be able to enter into depth,
never be able to seek the comfort of that deeper meaning — is this the world
we will have to live in from now on? I stood among those clean, white, flat
surfaces and couldn't stop myself from shivering. It made me feel so weak,
the thought of our total inability to change the world. We fail to obtain what
we want, in our pursuit of love or affection, and then we retreat to our separate
rooms. These days I keep hearing all manner of sounds in my head. There
seems to be such a full world in there. Thank you for the comfort you gave
me. I dare say you were right. But then again, I often wonder how much one
person can understand another. Words are so fragmentary, so self-
contradictory. Words are such fickle symbols: can we ever believe them
absolutely? I am gradually writing fewer letters now. I know that you and I
are not on opposite sides, but still, I also know that I can never give up the
part of me that wants to be me, I can never quite accept the way you try to
change things and make life easier for me. I talk about being me, but do I
really know for sure what sort of person I am? It's all words... I like to shut
the windows. Sometimes I turn off the light as well, and in the darkness it*

feels as if I'm in a cellar or a cave. You people may say that in this changing world there are many things more important than the feelings of an individual, but please, just think of me as a wounded animal which needs a long time to lick its wounds before it can recover. Don't be surprised if I don't write again. Once the light is off, I am the nameless chaos, I am the writhing in the dark, the multitude of things buried beneath the ordered light of day, of things lost in the relations of normal life. There, in that darkness, I possess my own imaginary world, a world that is both independent and strangely fruitful.

A man and a woman stand on the quayside by the railings. Behind them, wisps of smoke are still floating up from the large temple, but the crowd of the faithful has disappeared. A row of Tanka women are sitting on the temple benches, peeling water chestnuts, their children squatting beside them. They peel off the dark brown skins and discard them, revealing the white flesh inside. Then they put them into their mouths and chew them. In front of the temple is a pile of litter, left over from yesterday's Tin Hau festival: red stubs of joss-sticks, sheets of pink paper, pieces of wood, cans of drink, sticky tape, a soaking wet mass of rubbish. Now that the excitement of the festival is over the quayside is deserted. No boats have come alongside for a long while. The couple stand there, a long way apart. The empty ground in front of them slopes down to the sea. It too is piled with litter, some casually dumped oranges and lemons rotting there, providing a few brighter spots of colour.

It was drizzling when we came out of the funeral parlour. The sides of the road were covered with broken blossoms, withered and faded, tossed into the gutter or sticking to the pale brown slats of the bamboo frames. The muddy ground was soaking wet, the rain was streaming down on our faces. I said to Mother, 'Let's get a cab here and go back.'

I hadn't expected him to die so soon. I'd been abroad for a few years, and I'd heard that he'd grown frailer since the last time I saw him. A few months earlier, on my way back from my trip to China, I showed my mother the photos I'd taken in various places on the Mainland. We got to talking about my great-uncle, his brother, who'd been at daggers drawn with him all their lives, and who'd died a few years previously. Our generation, my generation, had grown up in a different world. For us meeting relations on the other side of the border was like meeting strangers. When Mother saw the children and the streets in the photos, she said, 'Goodness, I wouldn't have recognized them.'

Behind the undertaker's some young people were squatting on the ground and stripping the flowers off the wreaths. The flowers were still bright yellow, and after they stripped them, they put them into baskets to be taken away and re-used. The relatives waited under the eaves until the rain let up, and then went their separate ways.

I bowed to him in front of the bier. I looked at his photograph, and I no longer felt the bitterness I'd felt towards him as a child. I believe he did have some kindness in him. When we were little he told us stories about famous literary and historical figures. Even his witty couplets and bits of classical poetry and prose no longer seemed so hateful. What was the point of blaming one individual for the wrongs I'd suffered as a child. I bowed to him once again. Now we had made our peace.

I turned off the TV — no, I didn't turn it off. What happened was that the picture suddenly disappeared: the students round the bonfire, the government spokesperson, suddenly became a jumble of endlessly shimmering snowflakes. I suddenly became aware of how far away I was from it all. Watching those constantly shifting white dots, I recalled the images which had been there, then had flickered and died. Or had I constructed the whole geographical space from a few fleeting shadows? There is no doubting the countless fragments of memory and desire which come bubbling up from the waves of darkness, to be transformed into confused scraps of dreams. The land in which I had so recently set foot had become something unfamiliar. In the end the truest thing of all is intense personal grief. But that is something that cannot be put into words. There was no way I could go on living at home. This time before I finally decided to leave, I went to see her once more. But all she said was: 'My boss likes working in the evenings. I've got to work with him, so I haven't time to talk to you now.'

How can I ever make you understand the way I feel? Living in the West, we find the sense of impermanence profoundly unsatisfying. Perhaps inevitably we attribute to the East certain human qualities of gentleness and kindness. But then one day when we do come back, when we rediscover that East, we find her weighed down by very real concerns, real worries, we find that she has to obey authority, is subject to its control. She may even look with worldly scorn on my naivety. I did actually understand all of this. And yet at the same time I thought I'd somehow be able to master my selfish subjectivity, I thought I could be more accommodating and tolerant, and that one day she would recognize me for who I was. But she seemed utterly unshakeable — she'd never change on my account, she'd never understand me. I often wonder if the image I had of her at the beginning, of a person so sympathetic and tender, if that too was something I made up. Like piecing together a rough collage of a world from higgledy-piggledy scraps of newspaper cuttings, from old bits of writing and photos plastered on the wall.

How should I reply to you, my friend?

From here the view is one of a commercial metropolis at dusk, tiny cars crawling along the street below, more than usually crowded because it's the evening rush hour. The cars inch their way painfully forward. Looking up, beyond the towering summits of the skyscrapers, we can see the hills and a few faint rays of light shining through beneath the grey blanket of mist, coating the tips of this ice-cold modern city with a layer of ethereal gold. But always there is a line of tall buildings in front of us, masking half our view of the hills, covering up part of the source of this light, the glass of one building reflecting the shadow of the next. You talk about hiding yourself in a cave, you say you *are* a cave, but in this city that's out of the question; there are too many kinds of entanglement. It is impossible to extract yourself from all the multiple connections and changes that are taking place.

Even if you were a cave, I still couldn't stop myself from coming and knocking on your walls. I must tell you. I saw her the other day. In a spacious coffee-shop fronting on the street, among the potted plants and the mirrors, suddenly I saw the familiar profile. Was this the person you've been thinking about all this time? She didn't look any different from the people all around her. You once said you couldn't understand how it was that she seemed so stern and so morally aloof, and yet also so very worldly-wise and snobbish. It was as if she possessed two mutually exclusive personalities. Well, I think she's probably just an ordinary person, nothing more. She seemed to be echoing whatever her companions said, going along with their views on things. Her one short remark was clearly quite acceptable to them, as they all nodded in agreement. She seemed to become aware that someone was watching her, and started fiddling with her hair in a rather self-conscious way. I turned round, not wanting her to get the wrong idea. I don't think she recognized me.

At our table, people were discussing the present political climate, and worrying that recent events might mean tighter restrictions, in which case the last few years, when things have been relatively relaxed, would have been to no avail, and all the progress that's been achieved could be reversed. This was the important issue we were all discussing. But a vague image of you still lingered in a corner of my mind, it wouldn't go away. I remembered how, one evening when we were overseas, you started talking with such enthusiasm about bits and pieces of literature you'd read over the past few years, about new ways of seeing things, about how futile it was to try and bring fantasy down to earth, about how introspection had the power to open up a new reality. It seemed to be a whole way of relating to the world, something that you were able to identify with. Now, though you've been away so long, it seems you're wanting to send yourself into exile again, wanting to go away to some new and distant place. But I still feel you're here, you're one of us. Your sensitive probing of language has influenced our faith in the words we habitually use. In love, you tried so hard to get to know the object of your affections. Your efforts came to nothing, but that doesn't mean that your personal emotions and the chaotic world of the subconscious can just be brushed out of the way, to create a tidy, well-ordered world. The self keeps bobbing up and down, between the checks and controls on the surface and the dense, chaotic blackness underneath. It can't be written off at a stroke. If *you* weren't there, things would be incomplete.

Your story is not yet at an end. I look at you from here, I look at you on that new, far-off continent, and it's as if you're on a distant island; and then I look round at the grim shadows in the interior, and this place too comes to seem like an outlying border island. When I was watching her that day, she stood up, but the girls beside her didn't move, so she sat down again; later they got up to leave, and at once she went out with them. What would you have thought if you'd been there at the time? The two of you were really only together for a very short while, weren't you? After that you had to rely on letters to learn about each other. Later on, perhaps because of the sheer distance between you, because you were on your own in a foreign country, because you are a man of an enthusiastic and optimistic nature, you projected onto her qualities of generosity, honesty and tenderness; and when you actually came together again the whole thing turned out to be extremely painful. I watched her as she walked into the distance, until all I could see was an empty flight of stone steps outside the window. Maybe we don't need to deny all desire, all aspiration, just because one focus of our ideals has proved a disappointment. And we should consider her point of view, too. At the time she may well have had serious doubts of her own. She may have been afraid that contact with someone from outside might harm her…. The trouble is, once the heart has opened, it is easily scarred, and those scars can never be completely erased…

The ship slowly makes its way through the water between the two hills. Someone is speaking into a megaphone. The passengers lean over the side to see if the bell struck in one temple really does ring in the other, and if the paper money lit in one really does send up smoke in the other. But as they pass by now they can only see that the temple on one side is busy and bustling while that on the other side has its doors closed and is deserted. The two temples are very close together, and although they are actually opposite each other they somehow give the impression of being linked. The shadow of the hilltop on one side falls on the island on the other. The island seems positioned in such a way that it is connected and yet constantly changing and drifting, watching from afar the infinite sea and sky on the other side. A complex and shifting landscape is revealed, as each side is viewed from the other, at various differing angles. The ship sails slowly away. He is about to point something out to her when suddenly he realizes she is not at his side. The ship sails slowly away. Then he looks back and sees her standing smiling beside him. The ship sails slowly away. He feels vaguely that she is no longer beside him, and hesitates, not knowing whether he should turn and look for her. The man with the megaphone is once more explaining the landscape ahead. The names of all the little islands and of the hills around them, stretching into the distance, are so familiar. Behind them, very faint in the background, are the mountains of the Mainland, the great continent. The weather is fine, there isn't a cloud in the sky. In some places the hills are distinct, in others they appear to be connected.

Postcolonial Affairs of Food and the Heart

■ *Translated by Chan Wing Sze and John Minford*

1.

Ah Lee stumbled into my bar just as it was getting dark, carrying a bag of some fruit or other, something he'd picked up down the road in Peel Street Market. I hadn't seen him for an age. He sat down at the counter and started crunching up the long narrow brown fruit. He offered me a bite. He kept on saying how long it had been since the bunch of us last got together. Perhaps we could meet up some time soon and have a bit of fun, perhaps on my birthday, which was coming up. I tried the fruit and thought it had an interesting taste, a bit like a dried longan. It had a biggish stone, and a crumbly skin — just like a longan, in fact. But curved like a bean pod. You could almost imagine it to be a cross between a bean and a longan. Some sort of love child.

All these years, I've never been in the habit of celebrating my birthday. Probably because my parents sneaked into Hong Kong illegally in the first place, so I was born at home and never even had a proper birth certificate. When I grew up and went to get my ID card, I couldn't understand English and ended up putting down whatever date it happened to be that day in the place where it said 'date of birth'. I've got a family birthday, worked out by the old lunar calendar; I've got the made-up one on my ID card, which I use for official purposes; and then, later on, my aunt calculated the solar calendar equivalent for my lunar birthday, using the tables in the perpetual calendar. (I've never checked her calculations. That one's only there just in case.) So altogether I've got three birthdays, for use on different occasions. I've always been pretty casual about the whole thing, as you'd expect from someone of my undisciplined and capricious nature.

Last year, not long after my bar opened, we'd all gathered there one night and were drinking and chatting, when somehow, somebody mentioned that Lao Ho, our lecturer friend, had the same birthday as mine (or perhaps I should say the same as one of my three birthdays). Anyway, when the day in question came round, we all ended up having a party in my bar. Everybody brought something different to eat: hummus, tapas, pasta, Portuguese duck rice, some sushi. Marianne brought a French dessert — and dragged along one or two French friends she'd met while travelling in Spain, who provided some great rap music. Lao Ho brought his American university colleague, Roger. (He'd separated from his wife, who had gone to live abroad somewhere.) And I had invited Lao Sit, the famous veteran food critic. Technically, the bar, which functioned as a hair salon during the day, was not licensed for food, but under Lao Sit's expert direction, we chopped up some spicy ox innards and cooked them. We then got a bit carried away and wok-fried some genuine pig's intestine stuffed with glutinous rice, cut into slices. (That's the dish known as Beauty's Face in the Mirror.) We improvised as we went along, using the shampooing basins to wash the vegetables, and the hairdryers to air-bake some cured fish. It was just before the Hand-over, and our totally over-the-top menu chimed in perfectly with the general hysteria sweeping through Hong Kong. On the one hand, we had these nightly TV shows inflicted on us, featuring patriotic songs, public displays of nationalistic pride and fervour; on the other hand, foreigners were holding raves down the cobbled alleys of Lan Kwai Fong, celebrating their fin de siècle. It was either tomorrow and nothing else, or no tomorrow at all. Whichever way you looked at it, tomorrow somehow seemed to have become a huge red-letter day in the calendar, the anniversary of either the birth or the death of something or somebody great. To me, all of this was simply a form of 'date' worship. Big dates mean nothing to me whatsoever. But anyway, during those Hand-over days, we couldn't help making pigs of ourselves in general, singing wildly out of key, falling madly in and out of love. Drifting helplessly, suspended in a state of floating weightlessness.

When I got up the following day, I had a splitting headache. So I put a sign up on the salon door saying 'Day Off'. The whole morning, I was absolutely parched. Mine was an unquenchable thirst. I searched for water everywhere. I even attempted to start putting my old kingdom in order after the night's revels. I had every intention of making a fresh start. But it was no good. I discovered that several excellent wines from my cupboard had gone missing. And that wasn't all. The special bottle Miko had given me had disappeared, too, and I hadn't even had a chance to open it. There I was in my desolate salon-bar, feeling extremely sorry for myself, searching in vain for a down-to-earth way of filling up the emptiness inside. The morning after that particular party was my own fit of 'postnatal depression'. It was also when I first began to lose interest in parties and bars altogether (even my own).

And now here was Ah Lee, a year later, back in my bar — my not very successful little bar – talking about another birthday party. I couldn't help feeling that by now there were too few of us, too little left after all those crazy parties — nothing but a few tattered shadows. But somehow life manages to keep us on the run. He was right. It *had* been too long since the last meeting of our circle of friends. It would be great to see them all again. I relented. Ah Lee suggested going down to Chiu Kee, a poky, dingy little dive on Whitty Street. I knew the place. I'd been there once recently. The food had a really wokky taste to it — all steam and sizzle and oil. In fact, to tell the truth, the cook was a bit heavy-handed (with the MSG). The last time, his cooking had made me want to gulp water all night. And anyway, I said, it really was rather filthy, just a few round stools, not a single proper chair with a back to it. And Isabel had gone to Vietnam. I certainly couldn't imagine ladylike Alice, or trendy Marianne enjoying it for a moment. For *you*, said Ah Lee, I know they'll go. So... He'd obviously spoken to them about it already. Despite everything, somewhere deep down, we all of us wanted to snatch a few moments of respite, something reminiscent of the good old days. As he went on talking, I realized it had all been Marianne's idea in the first place. And it had been quite some time since she and I had last seen each other.

I remember the first time Marianne came in for a shampoo. She lay back with her head tipped upside down in the basin, looking like a proper grown-up woman. (Most of the time — as I found out later — she looks like a little girl.) What a strange mixture she was! I never could guess her age. She told me she worked at the Peninsula, but I couldn't picture a girl like her working in Hong Kong's smartest and most venerable hotel. It turned out she didn't know much about the place. For instance, she was not aware that when the Japanese invaded Kowloon, the British troops turned the Peninsula into their wartime headquarters and installed anti-aircraft guns on the top floor, pointing down Nathan Road. When I told her this, her upside-down eyes grew large, as if she was listening to some magical tale from the Arabian Nights, and her upside-down mouth opened wide. 'You talk just like my papa!' she said. I couldn't tell if she was flattering me or making fun of me.

Of course, I don't know the whole story of that period. I picked up little anecdotes like that from Lao Ho, the history lecturer. Lao Ho has very special hair. He's started losing some of it in the past few years. He hasn't been able to withstand this inescapable part of historical necessity. I've known Lao Ho for many years, and I've watched him going steadily downhill. In my daily line of work, I encounter all sorts of hair: dull hair, shiny hair, oily hair, layered hair, thick hair, hard-as-wire-wool hair, soft-as-silk hair, hedgehog hair, fox hair, shoe-brush hair, noodle hair... I've come to understand that hair doesn't necessarily reflect the personality of its owner. A lady from a rich family doesn't necessarily have luxuriant hair, nor does a university lecturer necessarily have academic hair, or an architect architectural hair. Not at all. In fact, I've been writing a newspaper column on hairstyles, fashion and food, and I've attracted quite a few readers. But Lao Ho is an altogether more rigid sort of writer. He sticks to serious subjects, and as a result he's been rejected by one newspaper after another. I was the first of us to start writing my own column, and stories of my own. I'd tried my hand at writing something once before, when I was a student. Now that I've got into writing again, after all these years, I feel the more I write, the easier it gets. But for Lao Ho, the hardest thing seems to be to sort out all the people and events to start with, to make any sense out of them. Like hair. Like a tangle of knotted hair. He just doesn't seem to know where to start.

Marianne and I started with hair. Or you could say we started (or ended?) with food. On the day of that very first shampoo, we discovered that we were both absolutely crazy about eating and drinking. We didn't just *like* eating and drinking; we were both of us prepared to go to the most enormous, almost fanatical, lengths to try out different places, explore new tastes, discover interesting new dishes. We were like a couple of stamp collectors or collectors of old books; we loved nothing more than swapping the latest tidbits of information with fellow addicts. For example, she once lamented the fact that there was nowhere one could eat rice-birds anymore. I protested that it wasn't true, that I'd eaten one just recently. 'No, no,' she murmured to herself, 'my papa says rice-birds aren't being imported into Hong Kong this year. There may never be another chance to eat them.' I promised her I could take her to a place that did rice-birds. That's how we ended up on our first date. We went out to eat rice-birds.

There were no flowers on our first date, no candlelight. It was more like two old gluttons meeting to swap tips on food and drink, not a man and a woman on a date. And yet, even in an old-style place like the Tai Hei Hing Seafood Restaurant, Marianne still managed to seem different — poised and in her element, in her Jil Sander outfit. We were surrounded by elderly businessmen, by whole families, grandparents, parents and children all together. It was a cheerful, rowdy sort of place. We opened the wine I'd brought. Marianne's taste in food turned out to be like an old Chinese gentleman's: rice-birds, dried larded pig's liver, black mushrooms, shark's fin. I wondered how she'd acquired her somewhat unusual ideas about food. Then she told me about her father. He was a real stickler when it came to food and drink. Apparently every time she went home for dinner, he insisted on setting an elaborate meal in front of her, to show off his culinary skills. And if they went out somewhere to eat, he was extremely critical. Nothing escaped his scrutiny. He showed no mercy. He was quite capable of sending back an entire dish, snorting and saying: 'Call this edible?' That night, when Marianne remarked that a dish was a bit on the salty side, I could almost feel the old man's phantom wheeling up above our heads.

When she went to study hotel management in France, her father still kept sending her package after package of food, she told me. A number of her earlier unsuccessful love affairs had somehow been connected with food, too. For example, she'd fallen out with one of her first boyfriends because he once suggested going to McDonald's. She just stood there in the middle of the road, staring at him in wide-eyed astonishment. '*What? You said what?*' Then she turned and stalked off. The most recent occasion had been during a Japanese meal. There'd been something very wrong with this last boyfriend's choice of restaurant. She sat there listening to everyone around the table praising the mediocre sushi, until she could stand it no longer. She just picked up her handbag, put on her shoes, opened the door and left. To this very day, that poor man still has no idea what the real reason was for their separation.

In fact, I've never been able to understand the way Marianne makes her mind up about things myself. That first evening she seemed quite impressed by the rice-birds, or maybe she liked the Bordeaux I'd brought. But the whole night I had this constant sense of apprehension that one of the old man's critical judgements might at any moment come popping out of this beautiful young lady's mouth. Luckily, she seemed to be in pretty high spirits. Especially when I told her that my hair salon transformed itself into a bar at night. She got terrifically excited about that and insisted on going back there afterwards to see the salon's other face. It was true. It did look totally different by night, with the big hair-dressing mirrors pushed back against the walls. In the dim light, they reflected the dimpled red lustre of the rows of bottles. She looked at my reflection in the mirror, as if she had suddenly seen me — her frog-prince. Then I think she turned and kissed me on the cheek. Someone had meanwhile broken the house rules and switched on the TV in the corner. I didn't know who'd done it, and didn't feel like enforcing my own rules anyway. They were broadcasting a firework show, celebrating something or other. Fortunately, the sound was off. I occasionally caught the subtitles; a song in praise of love, blood thicker than water, everlasting love, motherly love… I wasn't the least bit distracted by the silent hysteria. Marianne and I were much too wrapped up in a serious conversation we were having about food, trying one bottle after another from my private collection. Meanwhile, I was vaguely aware that the customers were drifting off. But I really can't remember what happened afterwards. I only know that the following morning we woke up together naked in bed. Like two people not connected in any way. I could feel her breathing on my chest, and her hands around me. But I couldn't remember what we'd done. I felt her gradually waking. Awkwardly, I tried to face the reality of ordinary life after the night's madness.

2.

I was a bit nervous when I first met Marianne's father. He was so formally dressed, in a way that made me feel more casual than ever. I'd suggested meeting in a newly opened French restaurant in one of the big hotels in Central, partly because I'd once been to a little place in London with the same name, partly because Marianne had never been there before. It was only after we'd made the arrangement that she told me of her father's connection with this particular hotel. He'd worked there for many years until his retirement, and still spoke frequently of its glorious past. Who knows, I thought, maybe the emotional link might even help the evening along. People are generally loyal to their golden memories of the past. Perhaps he might be less fussy as a result.

When Marianne introduced me, I got the vague impression she wanted to present me solely as the proprietor of a bar. She almost seemed to be concealing the fact that I was a hairstylist. It made me feel a bit like a bat, or some weird shape-shifting beast with certain unmentionable characteristics. And I'd come to think she liked me for being what I was, versatile, amphibious — like a frog!

It soon became obvious that even though the three of us were physically sitting in the same restaurant, we were thinking about totally different things, we were living on different planes. Marianne was dreaming of her wine-and-cheese experiences in Paris, and talked about the jamón and chorizo she'd recently eaten in Spain. I was thinking of my hippy days, when I'd studied hairdressing in London. At first, I'd stuck to Chinese food in Chinatown, but gradually, as I gained more confidence, I ventured out a bit and tried some other places around London. I could still recollect Isabel had taken me to that wonderful fusion restaurant near Hyde Park, to try their very distinctive cuisine. As for Marianne's father (who, it turned out, had been quite a big shot in the food and beverage section of this very hotel for years and years), he was needless to say recalling at some length the splendid days of his past, when Hong Kong had been the *real* Pearl of the Orient. He still remembered the grand opening of the hotel in 1963. He remembered the original swimming pool on the top floor, just behind where we were sitting, and how it had been demolished and rebuilt. He remembered the French restaurant that had been here in the old days, with its classy dark-green décor. (Where our table was had been the kitchen in those days!) Past the table where the Right Honourable Anson Chan (wearing a bright cheongsam) was sitting with her foreign guests, if you looked through the window beyond them, it was still possible to make out the shimmering harbour lights. But those golden days were well and truly over. The room was no longer the quiet sanctuary it had once been, the guests weren't so formal and distinguished, there was no lettering on the wine glasses. Even the waiters poured the wine with less panache. For the old man, who yearned for the style of the old days, nothing seemed quite right anymore.

My memories were so different. Unlike Marianne, I'd never spent the summers of my youth going swimming in the hotel pool on the top floor. I'd never tried the speciality lamb chop in the VIP room. I didn't have tooth decay from eating too many helpings of the delicious chocolate mousse served in the hotel cake shop. I had a number of unresolved questions of my own to ask the old man. Such as: How do habits of eating change? How do we explain the change? How does a whole way of life evolve?

He, meanwhile, was explaining why there was no lettering on the wine glasses anymore. His hair was tidy and slicked back. You could tell he was the clever type from his pointed nose and his sharp lips. After all his years in the hotel sector, he was a real expert and held forth about various aspects of the business, mentioning names: purchasing, expenditure, and of course, management. He told this story of how the three managers responsible for the purchasing and catering sections in such and such a hotel had made a fortune...

Marianne's father was a true member of the older generation. A man with principles. I wanted to ask him ... What *did* I want to ask? More about the history of the hotel? Which members of which royal family had stayed the night here? Which presidents and VIPs had held banquets here? About the vanished brilliance and splendour of the past... A Japanese woman correspondent who'd previously lived in Hong Kong had perhaps touched on the truth, when she once somewhat over-emphatically observed that she had seen a waitress in this very restaurant actually half take her shoes off! The implication was that from that precise moment the deterioration in Hong Kong's quality of life had become tangible. No, on second thoughts, I know that's not true. There are no easy answers, no formulae like that to explain things away. Take another, more upbeat, version of the 'truth', that the old privileged sanctuaries of Hong Kong had gone at last, were no longer the preserve of the elite, had been 'opened up to the common people...' No, that definitely wasn't the truth either.

I looked at all the other guests enjoying their food around us, the yuppies and the senior executives. Why *had* I chosen this hotel? Had I been searching for something else? I certainly recalled that wonderful restaurant in London, trying one interesting dish after another with Isabel. They had created such a beautiful combination: French cuisine and Thai seasoning. The experience had convinced me that East and the West *can* cook together, they can merge: Tom Yum Kung soup turning itself into a sauce for something else, French pastry wrapping itself lovingly round an oriental dish. No, I can't remember any more details. But it's true, I yearned for the taste again. Whatever it was, I remember it as being something exquisitely fresh. Sometimes I almost seem to catch the aroma still wafting through my mouth. Or maybe that's just a mistaken fantasy of mine? Why do I always forget? Why can I never find the words?

I took a bite of the puffed rice-cake in front of me, dipped it in a mild curried peanut sauce, and ate it. (I made a mental note: surely they should have added a little ham, garlic, and white wine?) I remembered eating it before, and it had definitely been tastier on that occasion. There was no point expecting Marianne's father to understand. He wasn't remotely interested in this common little snack sitting in the silver dish in front of him. (In his mind, it was probably nothing more than a few glorified peanuts.) He was so excited by what he was saying himself, his eyebrows positively danced as he talked about the old traditional dishes — abalone, sea slug, shark's fin and fish bladder. He knew how to tell a good shark's fin from a bad one, and a good abalone from a mediocre one. He was reminiscing about eating one of his favourite sorts of shellfish — poached conch: how stylishly the waiters used to slice it up, just a very few slices, and then serve it with a grand flourish. Pretty serious stuff. Frankly, I'd never even tried it. I didn't even know what it was. And I couldn't see what the big deal was anyway. What was the point of having all those extra waiters hanging around?

Marianne's father clearly wasn't interested in us at all. He made it clear he thought any person who considered puffed rice-cake edible an absolute fool. As for wasting good money on all this nouvelle cuisine, a pathetic sprinkling of vegetables, a few measly beans arranged on the plate — what ridiculous nonsense! (He was starting to sound just like one of his pretentious food-critic friends!) I had no idea what was actually going on, deep down in his mind. But I could tell I'd got it wrong once again. Wrong company, wrong food. It's a mistake I keep on making.

Fortunately, the red wine we ordered was passable. 'Mm... Saint-Emilion, pleasant bouquet.' The old man nodded approvingly. His French-educated daughter, the rebel, my mischievous Marianne, couldn't stand the airs her father gave himself on subjects she was infinitely more familiar with herself. 'I think I taught you that!' she taunted him. Her father, with his usual smiling composure, dismissed this little challenge curtly. 'Or maybe *I* taught *you*!' His briefly threatened dignity was thereby instantly restored.

To us, her father's authority was unchallengeable. He had this great mass of history stored away in his pocket. 'Now, how do you think a good dish of rice noodles with egg should be fried?' he'd say. This was the sort of question that clearly had a proper answer. It was utterly pointless my trying to display any intelligence on a subject I knew nothing about. Far better let the old boy hold forth, and listen. There was a story behind it — inevitably. An anecdote about the time when he'd been in charge of the Chinese food section in another big hotel in Central. His boss at the time, a certain Mr. Fu, was particularly fastidious about food. Fu went downstairs one night to have a snack before going to bed, and ordered a dish of fried rice noodles with egg. 'You see,' Marianne's father said, 'to fry a good dish of rice noodles with egg, the layers of noodles have to be spread on the wok one by one and fried over a high flame till both sides turn yellow. But that night, the chef doing the rice noodles was a bit careless, and when they were served, the noodles were still white. Mr. Fu took one look at the dish and flew into a rage. He took two bites, put down his chopsticks, then sent for Head Chef Chow. Actually, Chow hadn't cooked the dish himself, but he had to face the music anyway. Hm.' Marianne's father paused. 'Chow was a very stubborn man, and slow to admit the error of his ways. "Mr. Fu," he protested, "surely you didn't hire me to cook fried rice noodles?" Mr. Fu's face darkened. "Ask your superior, Mr. Fung, to give me a call tomorrow," he said. He was referring to me,' explained Marianne's father. 'So later on I called Chef Chow and spoke to him. "Don't you realize? You were hired as Head Chef. That means you're responsible for *everything*. Everything, however big or small. Even frying rice noodles. The tinier a thing it is, the more you have to be in command of the situation, the more you must discipline your troops."'

We were both a bit intimidated by the old man's introduction of military terminology and kept silent. Authority and tradition, when they join forces, can succeed in mowing down everything in their path. Of course, his rebel daughter had over the years acquired a certain immunity from this sort of onslaught. But still, even she stayed well away from the front line and kept out of trouble on this occasion. She let her father divide up the starter — goose liver — which he did in a most gentlemanly fashion (at that moment I remembered thinking how unbearably uncouth I must have seemed by comparison, a person who knew not the first thing about manners). The old man informed us that he didn't want much of the dish himself, it was too high in cholesterol. We went on to share all of the main dishes: a so-so duck breast, some overcooked lamb, a middling salmon. Marianne's father didn't say so explicitly, but I thought I knew what he was thinking: none of this could compare with the stylish French restaurant that had once been situated here on the top floor of the hotel. As for me, all the time I was eating the goose liver, I was constantly searching for that elusive Asian flavour I remembered from last time — that perfect blend of mango and ginger sauce … Where had it gone, where could I find that wonderful French-Thai hybrid I remembered from the London restaurant? Why couldn't I taste it here in Hong Kong? Those East-West recipes, that French tang with the cheeky Thai bite, they still haunted me, they still seemed to linger in my mouth. But had they really existed, or had I simply imagined them? Were they simply part of a postcolonial cuisine that existed only in my mind?

I would never have thought it possible to deny that Thai quality. But the waitress at our table, though she kept smiling, disagreed with me quite forcefully. 'Ours is definitely not Thai food, you see,' she said. 'It's French nouvelle cuisine, with a broadly Asian influence.' Oh dear. Once Thailand had had a character all of its very own. Now it had suddenly become 'broadly

Asian.' This was probably because we were in Hong Kong. Here, Thailand was no longer the mysterious, exotic Orient, as seen from afar, from distant Europe. It was no longer Siam. Seen from here it was stripped naked: Pattaya, bathhouses, hookers, and AIDS! (At that moment I could see one of the distinguished foreigners sitting at the table with Anson Chan — the lady we used to call Chief Secretary, but must now call Chief Secretary for Administration — looking at the harbour lights through the window as he enjoyed his meal. What kind of Hong Kong did *he* see in his mind's eye?) French cuisine has been very much the trend in the Hong Kong restaurant trade for the past few decades. Just as the old man said: that's where the real money is. You can't make any money out of Thai food. And, of course, in his mind, real French cuisine was supposed to be stylish, like the old Pierrot restaurant on the top floor. Very different from his daughter's bohemian memories of red wine and cheese. Marianne's father missed the dazzling silverware. I, for my part, was still dreaming of my original tropical Asian mango, with its wild, tangy ginger sauce, served side by side with the very best goose liver — everything called by its own proper name, everything on an equal footing. So there we were, the three of us, sitting around the same table, each thinking of a different kind of food.

All in all, that dinner wasn't much of a success. The condescending old man never actually complained, but his daughter registered his implied dissatisfaction. The two of them smoked cigars after dinner. (Marianne told me with some pride that her father had taught her to smoke cigars, as a way of scaring men away.) While they smoked, I was relegated to the role of her mother, who had always been, in Marianne's own words, an ordinary woman with no knowledge of the culture of food and drink. Like her, I was now just a non-speaking extra, supporting the true epicures, father and daughter.

I walked Marianne home, and somehow we started quarrelling. I can only remember that we were following the tramway, past a row of brand-name fashion boutiques with their vague, dark, bare mannequin shapes looming in the windows, when she began criticizing what I was wearing.

'You call that fashion? Let me tell you...'
She tugged at the T-shirt I was wearing under my jacket.
'Look at this! You really let yourself down!'
I felt angry and betrayed. I walked her up the slope and to the front door.
I watched her open the door and go in. Then I turned and walked away.

3.

A week later, Marianne came to my salon to have her hair done, just as if nothing had happened, and afterwards we went off cheerfully to have a drink. She always knew where the latest restaurants and bars were. That day we went to a newly opened bar in Wan Chai. Upstairs they served food, downstairs was drinking and dancing. I couldn't stand the Australian waiter's attitude upstairs, he was so snobbish and affected, so I went downstairs to drink. Probably I was a bit uptight. I started talking about the recent article in the *South China Morning Post* about discrimination against non-Caucasians in Wanchai bars. They were happy enough to welcome Asian women. But if you were an Asian man, they shut the door on you and pretended the bar was full. It was outrageous! Marianne was rocking her body to the music, really grooving to the rhythm. She didn't really agree with me and replied thoughtlessly, 'What's so surprising about that? It's always been like that!'

I was shocked by her attitude on that occasion, but afterwards we still kept in touch for a while. Even after we separated, I had to admit that she was great to be with. She was so lively, so full of ideas on how to have a good time. With her, as they say, you were never bored. And she was so kindhearted and easygoing, which was a rare quality. But occasionally she seemed quite bigoted. Her views on quite a number of things were positively unreasonable, stubborn, almost like an old man's. '*That woman*,' she'd say, 'she knows nothing about cheese!' It was as if the prejudices of some bigoted hundred-year-old man had percolated into her body and were speaking out of her mouth. I wondered who she was talking about. It turned out to be her mother! Every time she mentioned her mother, she just called her *that woman*, as if she were talking about a stepmother. Sometimes she talked about the delicious food her father had brought home from his hotel, or how he'd shown off by cooking her one or two mouth-watering dishes. She always used to say how *they*, 'Dad and I,' had enjoyed the food and bantered with each other. Her mother never managed to keep up. She enjoyed ordinary buffet meals, just as she enjoyed playing mah-jong and reading the gossip magazines. From Marianne's drunken, exaggerated description, I could just imagine the two of them, father and daughter, with their goose liver pâté, their oysters and lamb chops, emptying their bottle of wine, then each of them with a cigar, sucking the smoke in and blowing it out again. The dishes would be left scattered all over the long table, while at the far end sat this wizened old ghost in worn clothes from the Manchu dynasty, alone, chewing her steamed minced pork with a little salted fish, and a bowl of plain rice.

We were back in my bar by now, half drunk, leaning over the counter and watching TV. I'd revised my rules bit by bit, from 'No TV' to 'Watching TV', from 'No Food' to 'Bring Your Own Food'. I'd gradually had to accept the reality of the situation. I remembered how once when we were in London, Isabel and I had talked about opening a bar once we got back to Hong Kong. It had seemed at the time like an excellent excuse for checking out a whole lot of other bars and coming up with a blueprint of our own. All I really wanted was to have my own place after I came back, so that I could earn a living and chat with my friends at the same time. But things had turned out in quite a puzzling manner.

That night we ended up just watching TV, the Hysterical Handover Show. Next to us there was a young couple eating satay in a polystyrene container from the Thai take-away next door, floating in oil.

'*That woman*'s going to a banquet just like that!'

Marianne's finger swayed as she pointed to the handover banquet being broadcast on TV. The host proclaimed the name of each dish in his finest cadence and intonation. The camera zoomed in for a close-up of the dish, and we jeered.

'Wow! *Joy to Hong Kong!* Yum!'

'Wow! *Prosperity in Unity!* Delicious!'

Apparently, all the teachers from her mother's primary school had also gone to one of these official parties. The dishes had ultra-nationalistic names, words, and images signifying good luck and an auspicious future — they had us in fits! *Glorious Flight!* turned out to be stewed shark's fin with chicken in brown sauce. *Smile July the First!* was a dish containing black moss and stuffed marrow with dried scallops. The centrepiece of the occasion, *Joy to Hong Kong!*, was nothing more than fried scallops and celery with macadamia nuts. And as for 'Prosperity,' in the dish *Prosperity in Unity!*, it was basically good old Prosperity chicken, chicken cooked in pastry. Each time when we identified the true culinary facts behind the grand-sounding names, we booed. Actually, they were all dishes that we all knew well. The monstrous hype surrounding them, and the hysterical booing they provoked, totally spoiled our mood for that evening.

The day before, the very same media celebrities who were at the banquet had been dolled up in their fashion gowns and suits, cruising around in sports cars or helicopters, chattering endlessly into their mobile phones. But now, they'd all done a quick change into Chinese costume, cheongsams and Mao suits. They sat there beaming greedily at the camera, with all those rich dishes lined up in front of them. They could have been on a programme like *Gluttonously to Japan* or *Why Is Thailand So Enjoyable?* Hong Kong media personalities seem fuelled by a boundless supply of adrenalin, and an insatiable appetite.

I found myself wondering if Marianne's mother would really have been capable of feeling in place at one of these banquets? I couldn't tell. I only knew that by this stage of the evening Marianne herself was decidedly drunk. She waved her left hand in the air and made yet another dismissive remark about *that woman*. Then she mumbled to herself: 'Let's get those French guys to play some music! Let's go over to the other side of the harbour now and join the rave!'

'Marianne, you're drunk.'

'No, I'm not. I could still cook you up a *Prosperity in Unity!*'

Miko came over and supported the tottering Marianne. They looked like sisters.

'I'll walk you home.'

Marianne's head was swaying back and forth.

At this very moment, a loud sizzling wok sound could be heard on the TV behind us. Somebody in the bar cried out, 'Where's Lao Sit? We need Lao Sit! We need the expert! He can tell us if they're cooking the authentic Chinese way!'

'No he can't! He's too busy helping Ah Lee with his new bar…'

That was how I discovered that Ah Lee was absent. That was how I first learned that the two of them were setting up a bar of their own. They never told me themselves. They'd even decided on the venue. Apparently it was on the very next street. Strange, that everyone else should have known about it, and that I was the only person in the dark. Just two weeks ago, when Ah Lee'd been fired by his Japanese company, I'd asked him if he had any plans, and he said he hadn't decided anything yet. Why had they hidden the truth from me? The others told me that their bar was about to open any day, and that tonight was the night they'd asked Isabel to go round and advise them on what drink to order. So that was why Ah Lee had been asking me all those casual questions over the past couple of weeks…

'Sichuan snacks are going to be their big draw! Imagine that! Selling Chinese snacks in a Bar! You've got serious competition now!'

I was stunned to hear this devastating piece of market analysis from Kwok Keung. This could turn into a deadly feud! I began to feel the bitterness of betrayal. I'd thought we were friends! When had this started? Why?

At this precise moment, some people came rushing into the bar, belting out some song. Marianne's French friends. She'd just rung them up to come along. Seconds later, they gathered her up and were gone again.

Suddenly the whole bar became extremely quiet. It took me some time to get used to the silence. Finally Roger, who was sitting somewhere in the corner, stood up and put on a Chubby Checker CD. Lao Ho was sitting there looking rather bleak, half asleep.

Marianne's colleagues, who'd come with her, stood up and were about to go as well. One of them, Ah So, heard the music on his way out, and stopped and talked to me about Billie Holiday.

Then I heard a clink. I turned around: it was Miko washing the few remaining glasses.

'Thanks!'

When she'd finished washing up, she came over to the counter to get her handbag.

'I've got to go too.'

I looked at her, didn't quite understand.

'I'm off to Singapore tomorrow. If it all works out, I'm moving my whole company there.'

Then she added, 'And I'm getting married this summer!'

I was surprised, but not too surprised. I came round and said, 'Congratulations!' I hesitated, she didn't say anything, and I didn't ask. She was the maturest one among us. She must have her reasons. I trusted her judgement.

She went to say goodbye to Lao Ho. He saw her out of the bar and waited with her for a taxi. It was late, and the streets were so quiet. I looked through the window, there was only one old lamp at the upper end of the slope, and even that lamp looked as if it was about to go out.

A taxi came. She gave him a bear hug before getting in. He stood there watching the taxi go down to the end of the street, turn, and disappear. Other customers were leaving too. I walked them to the door. By then Lao Ho had walked up the slope and was gone. Everyone had left. I stayed there for quite a while. The night was growing cold. I turned into my bar and pulled down the iron grille.

4.

I spoke to Marianne on the phone, about the birthday reunion. It was quite some time since we'd last been in touch. It was weird. The passion had gone out of our relationship, but our interest in each other's day-to-day eating experiences was as keen as ever. It had survived unscathed. Marianne told me she'd originally suggested to Ah Lee going to Benissimo, an Italian-Sichuan restaurant, for the party. She'd been there recently and said the starters were particularly good. But apparently Ah Lee had said I wouldn't like it. I protested to her. I wasn't fussy. As a matter of fact, I enjoy poky, dingy places like Chiu Kee just as much as the more comfortable foreign restaurants in Lan Kwai Fong. That's me. Benissimo didn't have its own liquor licence, Marianne went on, so we would be able to bring our own wine. That was a definite advantage. We wouldn't have to go searching for somewhere else to drink after we'd finished eating. We could carry on there till it closed. In the end I talked Ah Lee round, and we went to Benissimo.

On the actual day of my birthday (I'll never be able to work out whether I was in fact born on that day or not, decades ago), Marianne rang me up at midday and asked to borrow a wok. She said they were going to make a risotto and asked me to join them for lunch. I brought my wok and some wine and once again climbed the stairs of the old Chinese-style tenement where she lived. Marianne came to the door, wearing a colourful kimono, a whimsical outfit, with a chopstick stuck in her hair. I recognized the old childish, gauche expression on her face. She was still the Marianne I knew, the zany girl who liked more than anything else to throw parties.

Two friends of hers were there. They'd both worked in hotels in Central, and recently, with the downturn in the hotel industry, they'd both lost their jobs. These days all the restaurants are looking for simple, economical menus, to tide them over the hard times. Ah So was there with some vegetarian goose he'd prepared, which was delicious. And Marianne? She cleaned the wok and produced her Heavenly Cookbook, a homemade scrapbook of recipes, written out in big bold calligraphy (perhaps her father's). She sliced some wild mushrooms and made a risotto, trying to stick closely to one of the recipes. There must have been plenty of ingredients missing, but we all ended up helping her, laughing, doing things any old how, mucking in, making it all up as we went along.

While we were having our lunch, the girls kept talking about what a terrible state the hotel business was in these days. Ah So told us that what used to be Chris Patten's favourite Italian restaurant was now offering a spaghetti lunch buffet for just over a hundred dollars. Karen said that was absolutely impossible, not in a classy place like that... They asked me what business was like in my bar, and I told them it had been a lousy year for me too. Not at all the romantic vision I'd had when the bar first opened. There were so many troublesome little things that had to be seen to. It was becoming more and more difficult to keep going. In fact I'd contemplated closing down, but then I thought I'd wait and see what happened in the coming few months.

The others left, and Marianne and I finished another bottle. It was odd. I hadn't seen her for several months, and yet she seemed more childlike than ever. Not at all the sort of woman you'd expect to see dancing the night away to a French DJ, not at all a woman capable of hurting someone like me. Just a little girl who loved parties – pyjama parties, hotpot parties. She was so innocent, you just accepted her as she was. You ended up thinking, this was the way she was supposed to be. There was nothing there to analyse or question.

Somehow I fell asleep. In my dream, a spell was being cast on everyone by a hundred-year-old ogre. Then Lao Ho started cooking. He made a dish of — ah, what was it? Not shrimp, not crab; whatever it was, he thought it was delicious and was asking everyone to try it, but nobody seemed to want any... Somebody had given me a brightly coloured box. I tried all the sides of the box, but I couldn't open it, I couldn't reach whatever it was that was concealed in its depths. Then I found myself tucking into the multicoloured reflection on the lid...

I woke up, and there was Marianne sitting on the bed I was sleeping on, chattering away on the phone. In French. They seemed to be talking about making soup. I went into the bathroom to take a shower, and after a little while, Marianne opened the door and came in. She just sat there on the toilet, right next to me, and chattered away about how to cook seafood soup.

The nap had revived me. That evening, at Benissimo, we sat around a long table. I was happy that all of these friends should have gathered together again after such a long interval. Right up to the last minute, Ah Lee and I had thought about switching to another place. He still had trouble with the idea of eating Sichuan food in a Western restaurant. I suggested leaving the final decision to the others. But they couldn't make their minds up either. And then somebody mentioned that we'd arranged to meet someone there — a mysterious friend — and that it was too late to contact this friend and change the arrangement. So we just stuck to our original plan.

I sat in the middle and looked at these friends around the table with all their different backgrounds. I reflected how difficult it was to reach an agreement on a matter as simple as what to eat and drink! I remember Isabel, who was sitting there opposite me, once telling me, 'Chinese food's so delicious. And it's even better when you can sit in a comfortable place and drink wine with it! Don't you agree?' She was right. It's always a real joy going out with Isabel to eat in Lan Kwai Fong. She's a true wine connoisseur and always brings excellent wine. But at the same time, I love wandering down the side streets and narrow lanes of Sheung Wan or Western District, with old gluttons like Ah Lee and Lao Chiu, dropping in at those grubby, shabby, dilapidated little places, sampling their unpretentious style of cooking. That sort of thing will disappear soon. And then there was our American friend, Roger, who is always rebelling against American food, and our Japanese friend, Miko, who was always rebelling against Japanese food. I'd had a great time eating with each of them. Somehow we seemed to have discovered the places that belonged to us, in different parts of Hong Kong. But now, even Miko the rebel, who had come to love Hong Kong, was planning to move her production company to Singapore. It was going to be harder and harder for all these people to get together again. Is there any kind of food that will suit all of these different people? Is there any kind of place?

My beautiful friend Alice was filled with conflicting emotions. In the past few months, all sorts of things had been declared unhygienic, unsafe to eat: chicken, seafood, pig's liver. The menu had crosses all over it, it was pockmarked, scarred, tied to the exigencies of the current situation. I reminded Alice what a long time it had been since she had given one of her excellent wine and cheese parties.

'It won't be long now!' she said. Even Alice had been hit by the recent slump in the stock market; she was all trussed up, like one of those live crabs they tie up in little bundles and sell on the street. Anyway, for her too, our gathering of friends tonight was a rare and happy occasion, so there was a smile on her face. She raised her chopsticks and tasted the three little starters they'd served. Things weren't so bad after all.

Somehow, I looked up, and saw Lao Ho's reflection in the mirror. He and I have the same birthday. He's my double. He just seems so depressed all the time.

Over in a corner, Ah Lee and Lao Sit had started kicking up a fuss.

'This is no good! What kind of Sichuan food is this supposed to be?'

'How can anyone call this Shadow Beef?'

These were the nationalists. The purists. Insisting on real Sichuan food in the cosmopolitan haunts of Lan Kwai Fong.

Over here, Isabel's champagne was finished. Downstairs, the bar couldn't find our white wine. Isabel went down to argue with them.

It turned out that Marianne had forgotten to give the wine to the manager, so it was still sitting at her feet. I took it downstairs and discovered Isabel acting as a barmaid. She was having a great time in amongst all the bottles.

When Isabel and I finally made our way back upstairs, they'd managed to call in the young cook, a labourer who actually came from somewhere in Sichuan. Lao Sit, as one would expect from a veteran food critic, was giving instructions in authentic Sichuanese dialect. He was insisting on some simple, standard Sichuan dishes.

Honda took out his video camera and started filming the chaotic scene. Ah Lee and Lao Chiu were taking it in turns to cross-examine the cook from the country, the one hired by the Italian proprietor. The results of his oral exam were pretty depressing.

'So you mean to say they don't even have the most basic chili bean paste from Pixian County!'

'And the chief waiter recommended us to have garoupa with chili bean sauce!'

Sitting opposite Alice was Kwok Keung the Analyst. He had finally stopped dissecting the achievements of the Chief Executive, the long-standing corruption of the cultural bureaucrats, the public mood in general, and the various reasons why the present election was unsatisfactory. He took up his chopsticks, picked up some suspect dry-fried string beans, popped them in his mouth, and chewed on them slowly.

We thought they were passable. But Ah Lee had other views.

'They aren't even dry!'

Roger, with the air of a philosopher lost in deep thought, helped himself to some sliced pork with garlic sauce and nodded approvingly. Ah So was sitting next to him. They were enjoying an animated conversation.

'No, no, no!' cried Lao Sit. 'What have they done with the pork? The one with garlic sauce hasn't any tang to it at all! And the one in soup isn't spicy enough! I can still feel the inside of my mouth!' He was swinging his head from left to right, like a spectator at a tennis match.

It was so strange. Ah Lee and Lao Sit had become the leaders of the debate, and the cook was behaving more and more like a jittery student. The more criticism he received, the more terrible his cooking became. It had actually not been that bad at first. But as time went by, in order to cater to his severe critics from the nationalist camp, and as a result of his ongoing interrogation, he tried to respond to some of their dubious comments and began throwing all sorts of different spices into the food. In the end, it was so hot it was inedible. And we ourselves were still wrangling about all the various culinary methods.

Luckily, just at this moment, events took a favourable turn (like the announcement of some long-awaited item of good news in the budget): the birthday cake arrived! Everyone settled down to celebrate our birthday, Lao Ho's and mine. Marianne kissed me, then Alice, then Isabel. Then they kissed

Lao Ho… Then suddenly someone announced: 'The Mysterious Guest!' It was Miko. She came in out of the night, straight from the airport with all her bags. We were all so excited.

'You're back at last!'

She smiled, 'Actually, I have to leave again tomorrow!'

Everyone squeezed along a little, and they added an extra seat. Someone suggested that Miko should sit beside me, but in the end they put her next to Lao Ho (she would probably be bored to death). She'd flown back just to see us, I thought I had to grab the chance to talk to her later.

It was time to cut the cake. It was my favourite white chocolate cheesecake. I was happy it wasn't dark chocolate, which was Lao Ho's favourite. It must have been Marianne's choice. She knew what I liked. When we arrived, she'd said she had to go to the laundry or something and had left a little earlier. She must have gone to the bakery!

Lao Ho and I cut the cake, and laughed at each other, at the different way we tried to cut it.

Marianne's French boyfriend arrived, too. I stood up and shook his hand. This was the first time we'd met, but there were no bad feelings. They're really an excellent pair. They go well together. Then a girl with a carefully placed 'designer hole' in her blouse came over to me from the next table.

'Happy birthday!' she said. 'I'm Ann. Doris is my sister. She knows you…'

'Right. But she's gone abroad, hasn't she?'

'I've heard that you're a good hairstylist. I'd like to come to your place and have my hair done some time.'

'This is my number.'

She held out her white little palm, and I wrote my number down on her soft skin. She gave me a mischievous smile in return.

I went back to my seat and looked around me. I was so content to see this jumble of friends sitting around one big table, chatting animatedly with each other, happily drinking up the wine. Some have left us and gone to live elsewhere. New ones have joined us. This is a difficult time for us all. We have different views on every subject under the sun. We argue endlessly. Sometimes we hurt each other a bit. But somehow we manage to stay together. Maybe in the end we learn to be kind to one another. The present situation is no good for any of us. It's late at night now. Outside the streets are empty and desolate. But we can still sit in here, we can still linger awhile amid the lights and voices, drunk on the illusion of this warm and joyous moment.

Afterword
Writer's Jetlag[1]

■ *Translated by John Minford and Agnes Hung-chong Chan*

You could say I've been a traveller all my life. A permanent migrant. My parents migrated from the 'continent', from mainland China, to Hong Kong in 1949. They were literature lovers who adored things like *The Story of the Stone*[2] and the new twentieth-century Chinese vernacular literature of the May Fourth Movement. They brought few valuables with them in their travelling bags. But they did carry loads of books. My maternal grandfather, like so many Chinese men of letters before him, retired to the seclusion of the countryside in a mood of profound disenchantment. He found some land in Wong Chuk Hang in the southernmost corner of Hong Kong Island, grew vegetables and raised chickens — a latter-day Tao Yuanming,[3] plucking *pak*

---

[1] Originally presented by Leung Ping-kwan at the Sinophone Literature Workshop, Harvard University, April 2006.
[2] Cao Xueqin, trs. Hawkes, D. and Minford, J., *The Story of the Stone*, Harmondsworth: Penguin Classics, 1973–86; see also Yang, X.Y. and Yang, G., *The Dream of the Red Chamber*, Beijing: Foreign Languages Press, 1978–80.
[3] Tao Yuanming (AD 365–427), prototype of the Chinese hermit poet, famous for the lines 'I pluck chrysanthemums under the eastern hedge,/And gaze afar towards the southern mountain' (from his 'Poem Written While Drunk', translated by William Acker, in Minford & Lau, *Classical Chinese Literature*, New York and Hong Kong, 2000: pp. 503–4).

choi under the eastern hedge and gazing afar, in not too leisurely a fashion, towards the less-than-attractive Brick Hill (Southern Long Shan).

My family's home in the country was humble, but it contained a treasure-house of books, a library that had drifted with them from the mainland to the small island of Hong Kong. They had works ranging from classical Chinese poetry and fiction to modern literature, from Lu Xun[4] to Zhang Ailing[5] to old Soviet fiction, from Zhu Shenghao's translated works of Shakespeare[6] to *The Guava Collection (Fanshiliuji)*, Zhu Xiang's[7] anthology of western poetry in translation. Besides the literary classics, there were plenty of popular romances too. When I was small and no-one was looking, I used to read these by myself, and then I'd while away the hours adapting the stories in my head, in my own random fashion. My grandfather was well versed in classical Chinese poetry, and he was also fond of expounding the intricacies of the cleverly constructed couplets and some of the witty puns perpetrated by outstanding Cantonese scholars of the older generation. My father, who died young, had forced himself to delve into some of the indigestible political theories of art and literature that were current at the time. But what I related to most of all as a child were my mother and her sister and their Cantonese recitations from memory. They chanted poetry and prose as they worked together, doing piece-work at home, assembling plastic flowers, pasting labels on matchboxes, or threading beads. And I specially loved reading the popular romances which my aunts kept for their regular leisure reading.

Before finishing primary school, I moved from the country to the city. I was amazed by the wonders and the vastness of my new urban environment, and at the same time continued to pursue my love for literature by reading more and more books in the city library. But nowhere could I find a point of reference in the 'reality' around me for the things I was busy reading about. My passion for Chinese books caused me to resist the prevailing trend, which

---

[4] Lu Xun (1881–1936), novelist and essayist.
[5] Zhang Ailing (1920–1995), prominent novelist, who 'migrated' from Shanghai in 1952.
[6] Zhu Shenghao (1912–1944) translated thirty-one of Shakespeare's plays into Chinese.
[7] Zhu Xiang (1904–1933), poet, critic and pioneer translator.

was to study in an English secondary school. Instead I entered a Chinese secondary school. My Chinese teacher, who came from Beijing, considered my experimental Chinese unacceptably odd and insisted that I should use the old-fashioned four-character clichés, in order to make my Chinese prose style seem more mature and fluent. I refused to do this, and as a result I always got a C minus for my compositions. My English teacher, by contrast, was very encouraging, and lent me a lot of modern fiction, which I read avidly. So when I finally got into university I chose the English department. But the syllabus turned out to be quite different from what I had expected — it was all Chaucer and Milton, or else it was American Literature taught by old missionary ladies. So I started skipping class and went to watch movies instead. In the quest to satisfy my ill-defined yearnings, in my search for a different kind of literature, I also scoured the bookstalls for the latest in foreign books and magazines.

Quite apart from what was going in school or at university, those of us who grew up in Hong Kong during the 1950s and 1960s benefited greatly from the variety of cultured individuals who migrated from the mainland to Hong Kong in that period: philosophers, educators, artists, creative people in the movie industry, and of course countless journalists and writers. They had differing political stances, but they each in their own way helped to create a vital link between Chinese language and culture, both ancient and modern. And what was unique was the fact that this was happening outside of China proper, in Hong Kong. The British colonial educational system and its syllabuses were certainly conservative, but we were lucky to be able to supplement it with lots of popular newspapers and magazines, which provided us with a knowledge of our own past history and culture, from a number of widely varying perspectives. During the 1950s, alongside the intellectuals and artists who moved from the mainland to Hong Kong — the neo-Confucian sages, the movie people, the writers and journalists from Shanghai and Guangdong — there were also many individuals dedicated to education and journalism, all of whom, in response to the specific social limitations of Hong Kong and its commercial environment, found themselves obliged to pay equal attention to highbrow and popular culture. The resultant fusion helped to provide us, the younger generation, with a new and broader understanding of the world we lived in. Take, for example, the new literature that had been emerging for several decades in China. New or modern literature of this kind had never been acknowledged by the official Hong Kong secondary or university curricula, but despite this we were able to find complete collections in secondhand bookshops, and it was common practice to produce anthologies of modern literature in Hong Kong — and even to bring out unofficial reprints of rare editions. Scholars like Cao Juren, Li Huiying, Sima Changfeng, Xu Xu and Jin Shengtan either wrote histories of literature or produced their own reminiscences of the literary world. Newspaper columns and special issues of magazines all provided a new generation of readers with a form of 'private tuition' on the subject of modern literature. A few exceptionally insightful writers, such as Liu Yichang from Shanghai, with his *Boozers* (*Jiutu*, 1963), or Ma Lang, editor of *New Wave Art and Literature* (*Wenyi Xinchao*,1956), even introduced us to other traditions beyond the May Fourth mainstream.

I began to write in the late 1960s and early 1970s, which coincided with the Cultural Revolution in the mainland. That particular political view of literature was very influential in Hong Kong, where the pro-China writers wanted to fly the flag of socialist critical realism. In my usual perverse fashion, I refused to join their ranks, preferring to go in search of new ideas from other parts of the world. As a port city, Hong Kong had the advantage of receiving a constant and sizeable influx of foreign books and magazines, which made their way straight to the news-stands of Central and Tsim Sha Tsui. I cut out ads and subscribed to underground magazines and hard-to-find reviews of books. I wanted to re-assess my own reality through the imaginative lens of the foreign world. I learned to write by doing translations into Chinese of new French fiction, American underground literature and Latin American stories. All of these were published in Taiwan. Meanwhile, I also made my own attempts at creative writing. In Hong Kong in 1972, my friends and I ran a new magazine called *Four Seasons* (*Siji*), which in retrospect is still a valid reflection of the literary ideas of the time. In addition to original writing, the first issue included features on Mu Shiying,[8] on the Colombian writer Gabriel García Marquéz, and on the Italian film director Bernardo Bertolucci, together with a translation of his 1964 screenplay *Before the Revolution*. There were also critical reviews of new foreign-language books and of new works by contemporary Taiwanese writers like Ch'i Teng-Sheng, Huang Chun-Ming and Shih Shu-Ch'ing. Literary thinking at that time had inherited the conventions of May Fourth literature, with its emphasis on original work, translation, criticism and cinema, but the difference was that our criticism focused on writers who at that time could not conveniently be introduced to other parts of the Chinese-speaking world, or else on writers that the Chinese world was slow to recognize. Hong Kong had a culture of its own, a culture that was different from the mainland. We were developing a tradition outside the May Fourth mainstream. Island and continent, again.

My interest in Latin American literature in the early 1970s arose out of my opposition to the literary atmosphere that prevailed in Hong Kong at that time: at one extreme, literature was dominated by politics, while at the other, fractured texts were appearing that stemmed from a purely modernist tradition in poetry that was internally driven. Latin American literature seemed to represent a more open and more fertile alternative, a way of attempting to write about an individual's inner desires and dreams, while at the same time dealing with the history, society and culture of that individual's country. In my first collection of short stories *Shimen the Dragon Man* (*Yanglongren Shimen*, 1979), I drew on magical realism to explore the absurd reality of Hong Kong. Later in my novelette *Paper Cuts* (*Jianzhi*), I continued to develop this style, probing into the question of why there were so many different, even conflicting, cultural strata in a single society.

Some pieces in my Chinese-language collection *Islands and Continents* (*Dao he Dalu,* 2002) were written when I was a student in America in the early 1980s. China had just gone through the Cultural Revolution, and was

---

[8] Mu Shiying (1912–1940), Shanghai writer of fiction.

starting to open up to the wider world. I personally had my first experience of studying abroad and living in a different culture. I had originally intended to look at the influence of classical Chinese poetry on contemporary American poets. Later I became more interested in collating the neglected works of Chinese poets from the 1940s (the foxed, pocket-sized collections of poems which had fortunately survived the flames of war, and which we had had the luck to read in our youth). In my treatment of this subject, I borrowed from Western discussions of modernism. Though I was living in America, I was sensitive to the changes in China, and had my first opportunity to live in contact with Chinese students from the mainland, Taiwan and elsewhere. Through our daily exchanges, we discovered each other's life-stories, and enhanced our ability to understand each other's experiences. I returned to Hong Kong in 1984, just as the British and Chinese governments were initialling the joint declaration for the hand-over of Hong Kong to China. I found myself in the midst of intense popular anxiety, surrounded by a general sense of angst. I experienced a new sense of personal disjuncture, a new variety of my recurring condition of cultural jetlag. I found it particularly difficult to readjust myself to the atmosphere of Hong Kong society; and at the same time I found myself wanting to look at all these cultural similarities and differences from a variety of angles. *Islands and Continents* was created against this background, in this atmosphere. I wanted to write about the connections that existed between various islands and various continents — the 'new' continent of North America and, the ancient mainland or 'continent' of China. Traditional culture was changing and developing in all sorts of ways, and in the twists and turns of modern history many novel and unusual stories were to be found. Different structures of emotion had arisen out of different backgrounds. In the strangely weightless state brought on by this state of temporal and cultural jetlag, I tried to look at both islands and continents: they were not necessarily mutually contradictory entities; continents existed within islands, and islands within continents. As a consequence, the stories I created were generally different from the prevailing modes of expression, from the patriotic hymns on the one hand, and the desperate elegies for a lost city on the other. My ideas differed from those of most people, and my style of writing became more and more outmoded, and out of tune with the times — I wanted to pay less attention to plot, and more attention to the day-to-day emotions of characters. Moreover, my fondness for poetry inclined me to attempt a type of fiction that was both cultural and lyrical. I don't believe that changes in one's life are brought about by dramatic events. I prefer lyrical fiction with its emphasis on the role of atmosphere and mood. I prefer its subtle and insinuating, but nonetheless powerful, effect. People have often maintained that lyrical fiction is best suited to the expression of personal emotions, but I like to think that it is possible to bring out something more than just private feelings: reflections on history and culture?

It took me ten years (from the mid-1980s to the mid-1990s) to finish my novel *City Remembered, City Imagined* (*Jiyi de Chengshi, Xugou de Chengshi*), a work which I started writing almost at the same time as *Islands and Continents*. The novel tells of several young people making their way back to Hong Kong from abroad. I had always had a keen interest in the travelogue genre in pre-modern fiction. Over and above that, I attempted to include in my novel a range of disparate elements: poetry, prose, experimental drama, monologue, visual art and critical discussion. As a result, I paid less attention to the plot, but was more interested in cultural encounters and negotiations. I wanted to experiment with an open narrative structure which could embody a fuller range of sentiments and thoughts.

I witnessed the crushing of the student movement in Beijing in the summer of 1989, and later that year I travelled to Eastern Europe to try to understand the changes that had taken place there. My contact with other cultures also offered me a new angle from which to reflect on my own. After my return, I added the short stories written during the trip to some I had finished earlier in Hong Kong, to form the book *Postcards from Prague* (*Bulage de Mingxinpian*, 1990). It includes pieces dealing with contrasting elements and with points of contact between different cultures, and touches on the various media that people of different cultures rely on to communicate with each other: the letter, the postcard, the telephone-call, the fax and the e-mail.

Writing in Hong Kong, we are inevitably situated (at one and the same moment in time) somewhere between refined (high) and popular (low) culture, and my stories have appeared one after another in different types of popular publication — a fact that I have no desire to conceal. On the contrary, I think it highlights the ambiguous relationship between popular culture and literature. But not all critics have been able to appreciate this, and I received both praise and blame for the book. One young writer criticized me for engaging in a totally unacceptable literary game, and urged me to learn from Lu Xun... Another critic actually considered the book 'immoral'. Later on, for some unknown reason, I received a biannual award for this very book. And then as time passed, no one talked about it any more.

I have recently been writing a series of stories entitled *Postcolonial Affairs of Food and the Heart* (*Houzhimin Shiwu yu Aiqing*), which will soon be finished. Nowadays, I find that working abroad gives me a welcome sense of distance. I grew up in Hong Kong and have a deep feeling of involvement with the place. But I have never gone along with value judgements or engagements of any kind. I constantly experience an underlying sense of temporal disjuncture in my life, I suffer from a chronic condition of cultural jetlag — even when living in my own society. In 'reality', I find that other people's clocks sometimes go a great deal faster than mine, sometimes a great deal slower. It's true, I write essays discussing Hong Kong culture and Hong Kong film. But I prefer to explore these issues through creation. The writing of fiction is a kind of instinctive exploration: it follows no theoretical framework, it stays close to life, and allows more freedom and openness by placing characters in specific or ambiguous situations. In Hong Kong I'm not considered a mainstream writer; but I am not thought of as totally marginal either. Publishing my work is not easy. There is less and less space for art and literature in newspapers and periodicals. Still, some people read what I write, even if the overall environment promotes different values. It's hard to promote the cause of literature, and there is little genuine criticism around. There are relatively few good critics writing in Hong Kong, a fact that we can do nothing about. We're free to write what we want, but people in general are more interested in other things. When I'm abroad I want to learn about foreign culture, and at the same time I often find myself defending Hong Kong. And yet when I return to Hong Kong, I always get angry, keep criticizing and arguing with others. It's no good being like that. It's better to concentrate on my story telling. I don't want to write about big political issues, just about human nature and people: how they eat, how they love.

Contributors' Biographical Notes

John Minford studied Chinese at Oxford and the Australian National University and has taught in China, Hong Kong and New Zealand. He edited (with Geremie Barmé) *Seeds of Fire: Chinese Voices of Conscience* (1988) and (with Joseph S. M. Lau) *Classical Chinese Literature: An Anthology of Translations* (2000). He has translated numerous works from the Chinese, including the last two volumes of Cao Xueqin's eighteenth-century novel *The Story of the Stone* and Sunzi's *The Art of War*, both for Penguin Classics. He has also translated *The Deer and the Cauldron* (2000-2003), a three-volume Martial Arts novel by the contemporary Hong Kong writer Louis Cha. He is currently Professor of Chinese at the Australian National University.

Brian Holton is currently teaching translation at The Hong Kong Polytechnic University. He has published several volumes of translations of Yang Lian's poetry, including *Concentric Circles* (2005), *Notes of a Blissful Ghost* (Hong Kong, 2002), *Where the Sea Stands Still: New Poems* (Newcastle, 1999) and *Non-Person Singular: Collected Shorter Poems of*

Yang Lian (London, 1994), as well as translations of Chinese literature into Scots, including *The Nine Sangs (Chuci Jiu Ge)*, several chapters of *Men o the Mossflow (Shuihu zhuan)*, and a great deal of pre-modern Chinese poetry.

Agnes Hung-chong Chan obtained her first degree in Translation and Chinese from the Hong Kong Polytechnic University in 1994 and her master degree in English Studies from the University of Hong Kong in 1997. She edited the first volume of 含英咀華, *A Chinese Companion to Classical Chinese Literature: An Anthology of Translations* (2001). She translated (with Brian Holton) Yang Lian's *Concentric Circles* (2005). She now works at the Centre for Translation Studies of the Hong Kong Polytechnic University.

Chan Wing Sze was a student of translation at the Hong Kong Polytechnic University. She is now a teacher of English at a secondary school.

Caroline Mason taught Chinese language and literature at the University of Durham, UK, for many years and now works as a freelance translator. She also teaches translation at the University of Newcastle.

Robert Neather studied Chinese at the University of Cambridge, gaining a PhD in Chinese literature there in 1995. He also holds a postgraduate diploma in translation and interpreting from the University of Bath, where he later returned to teach. He is currently an Assistant Professor at City University of Hong Kong, and teaches various courses in the Chinese translation programme. His areas of interest include literary translation and the use of translation in museum display.

Shirley Poon studied Translation and Chinese in the Hong Kong Polytechnic University and obtained a scholarship to study English and Linguistics at the University of Durham. She received her MA in Translation and Interpretation in 2004, and is now pursuing another MA in Applied

Linguistics. 'Romance of the Rib' is the second piece she co-translated and published with Dr. Robert Neather.

Shuang Shen, an Assistant Professor in the English Department of Rutgers University, is the author of a number of articles in both English and Chinese on Chinese diasporic literature, Hong Kong literature and film, and Asian American literature. She was a co-editor with Leung Ping-kwan of a special issue of 'Literary Review' focused on Hong Kong literature. Currently she is working on a book project on English-language magazines and cosmopolitanism in the semi-colonial city Shanghai.

Jeanne Tai was born in Hong Kong but now lives in Cambridge, Massachusetts, where she occasionally dabbles in translations.

Tong Man, Jasmine received her BA (Chinese, Translation and Interpretation) and PhD (Translation) from the Hong Kong Polytechnic University. She taught in the Language Centre of the Hong Kong University of Science and Technology from 2001 to 2003. Currently she is a Teaching Fellow of the Department of Translation at Lingnan University in Hong Kong.